AUSTIN TRANSLATION

Austin Translation
by
Zach Selwyn

Book One of *The Stoner Chronicles*

ROGUE MATTER
Chief Business Officer - **Christopher W. Yan**
Chief Creative Officer - **Michael Dolce**
Editor-In-Chief/Wrighter of Wrongs - **Trent Olsen**
Senior Director, Strategy - **Heather Knapp**
Consulting Editor - **Renae Geerlings**
Head of Product and Technology - **Rogerio Lemos**
Creative Assistant - **Karla Luiza**
Executive Producer - **Taz F. Stark**

GUNGNIR
Founder & Publisher - **Mathew Medney**
Executive Editor - **Steve Orlando**
Editor in Chief - **Jim Krueger**
Senior Designer - **Mohamed Samah**
Narrative Director - **Alex Kane**
Operations - **Ed Aldana**

Rogue Matter is a distributed Publisher of Macmillan through the Gungnir network.

The Stoner Chronicles, Book One, Austin Translation. February 2026. © 2026 Rogue Matter, Inc. All Rights Reserved. Editorial offices: RogueMatter, 750 S Bundy Drive, #108, LosAngeles, CA 90049. Rogue Matter, the Rogue Matter logo, and the The Stoner Chronicles Series logos are TM and © 2026 by Rogue Matter, Inc. All Rights Reserved. Any similarities to persons living or dead are purely coincidental. With the exception of artwork used for review purposes, none of the contents of this publication may be reprinted without the permission of Rogue Matter Inc.

Find ROGUE MATTER online:

website • **roguematter.com**
facebook • **facebook.com/wearroguematter**
instagram • **instagram.com/wearroguematter**
youtube • **youtube.com/roguematter**

Printed in Canada

FOREWORD

By Kinky Friedman

When Zach Selwyn first sent me this manuscript, I told him it would probably be the "greatest novel I'll ever pretend to read." But then I actually sat down and read it. Selwyn's novel *"Austin Translation"* is one of the best books I've read since Christ was a Cowboy. He writes with a ruthless economy of words yet the characters seem to leap off the page. Selwyn's voice comes through like a train whistle in the night and it makes *"Austin Translation"* a joy to read. My only concern is that this book may encourage even more humorless, constipated, tedious Californians to move to Texas. I myself, whilst reading Selwyn's book, felt a strong urge to move to Texas - then I realized I was already here. As the great mystery writer Raymond Chandler once observed, "Scarcely anything in literature is worth a damn, except what is written between the lines." That is where Zach Selwyn does some of his best work.

CHAPTER 1

It was one of those obnoxious, hipster hotels.

You know the type. The rooms have rotary dial phones in them that are only capable of reaching the front desk. You can rent a vintage typewriter for $50. 00 if you feel like composing some longhand poetry. Each room has a sewing machine. They refuse to use electronic key cards in the locks, so you are provided with a ridiculous oblong 1970's-era key chain that costs $15. 00 to replace and guarantees you will lose it within your first 24 hours... It was one of those places with its own merchandise table.

Welcome to the Hotel San Joaquin in Austin, Texas.

I had flown into town that afternoon to record an episode of a true crime podcast with my business acquaintance and newfound friend Pete Vreeland, a journalism professor at the University of Texas at Austin who had recently convinced the school to give up teaching 1970's-era journalism and focus on new media ventures, such as podcasting. It was a brilliant move, and the "New Media Journalism" had suddenly become by far the most desirable major for hundreds of UT undergrads. In Vreeland's program, students write, edit and create their own podcasts and distribute them across streaming platforms. It was a new way of creating content and Vreeland knew that he was sitting on motivated kids who would work for free. At least until they graduated.

In the previous year, two of his students had actually solved a cold case murder that had taken place in Austin 25 years earlier. The podcast, which was called The Lemon Grove, constantly charted in the top 20 of the "true crime charts" and had brought a lot of attention to UT Austin's program. As well as to my podcast company, DETAIL, which had decided to partner with Vreeland on future endeavors.

Flying to Austin couldn't have come at a better time, as we were in the dog days of summer back in Los Angeles. My wife and I weren't talking… again. Or if we were talking, it was an argument about laundry, our son's lack of interest in anything but video games and where to properly put the mustard back into the refrigerator. Typical we've-been-married-for-15-years kind of stuff. On top of that, three weeks ago, my wife had asked me to move to the spare bed in my son's room. A week later my son asked me to move to the bunk bed in my daughter's room. Three days after that my daughter then asked me to move to the living room couch.

Luckily there was no one left to throw me out any further.

I wasn't sure how my marriage had gone south, but like a lot of couples during the quarantine of 2020, the constant daily head-butting had taken a toll. There were no gyms for people to escape to, no offices to hide in and no lunch meetings. For seven months, it was basically the same thing day in and day out. Coffee. Food. Struggle to get the kids to do their home-school assignments. Wine. Netflix. Bed.

A few of my friends' marriages had crumbled during the Covid-19 pandemic, and every time I spoke to the beleaguered husband as I helped them move their stuff from their Bronson Canyon houses into one-bedroom apartments in Koreatown, it was the same conversation:

"We just couldn't agree on anything."

"We just bickered all the time."

"She fucked her masseuse."

Masseuse or not, marriages were decaying faster than the banana I had packed for the flight that I had just pulled from my backpack. I settled in to check some emails before meeting Vreeland for a drink. One particular email caught my eye and it was from an old musician acquaintance named Alfie Adams:

Hey Rob, hope this finds you safe during this pandemic. Not sure if you remember me, I was the bass player in Roadflowers when we opened for you on tour in Europe around 2003. Anyway, I have something of yours that I think you'll be happy to see. I'm in Austin, so happy to meet up - just let me know where you're staying.

Hearing from Alfie after 17 years was certainly strange. What was even stranger was that he knew I was in Austin. Even stranger, was what he said in the email. He HAD something of mine? What could it be? An old guitar I had lost on that European tour? Money I was owed? God forbid he had a child that he thought was his but happened to be mine... I needed a drink.

The pool at the Hotel San Joaquin always has people in it casually sipping mixed drinks and talking about music. In my younger days, I would have been there with them, arguing over which was the best Lightnin' Hopkins album or something, but at 7:00 at night my heart was set on the lounge.

That's where I met Casey Dixon.

Wearing a mask hides many people's worst facial features, so at this time in the world, when we are all required to have a mask on indoors, eyes are the most important and dominant feature we recognize. Casey had mesmerizing eyes. Like, cerulean blue. Clear and alive. As I ordered a $14.00 glass of Rioja, I complimented her on them.

She complimented me on my mask.

My mask was made out of some strange blue fabric that was left over from when my wife had spent $250 re-covering our couch cushions a few months earlier. I know she resented the fact that her perfect couch cushions - which she had spent all this time covering and designing - had become pillows on my makeshift bed for the past few weeks, but the extra fabric had made a pretty cool looking mask.

Casey was basically "mask-flirting."

I went to the outside bar and drank my wine before Vreeland came sauntering in, already three drinks deep. He was happy to see me, as his marriage was teetering on disaster as well and he took my quarterly trips to Austin as his get-the-hell-out-of-the-house moments. And, as he pointed out, he was "working" by meeting with me.

Of course, working with Vreeland meant drinking, and we made our way out of the hotel and over to Stereo, a hip outdoor cafe/restaurant/beer garden a mile and a half up the road. Austin is full of these places. Stringed lights, craft beer and everyone wearing what I call Generic-ana. Flat brimmed cowboy hats, turquoise rings and snap shirts. Basically the same outfit I was wearing on that 2003 European tour with Alfie Adams and the Roadflowers.

As the beer flowed, Vreeland relayed new university podcast information to me, asked me if my company would get behind a show about a former UT football legend and we commented on the number of beautiful women encircling us. At 45, I was no young man, but I looked young enough to convince someone I was possibly 37. I chalked my youthful appearance up to red wine and sunscreen.

Buzzed, I left my rental car at Stereo and took a Lyft back to the Hotel San Joaquin. Vreeland went home.

When I walked in, I expected the bar to be hopping - after all it was Friday night and pandemic or not, Austin had a nightlife to uphold. However, the place was deserted. I soon found out that they closed at 10: 00 due to Coronavirus. The only person in the lounge was Casey Dixon, wiping down her counter.

"Hey, it's the cool mask guy," she said as I walked in.

"Hey, it's the mesmerizing eyes girl," I repeated.

"You want a glass of wine?"

"I'm good," I said. "Not trying to spend any more money tonight."

"On the house..."

Casey joined me in the outdoor beer garden and removed her mask revealing full lips, clear skin and a perfect smile. She was beautiful. I took mine off as well... revealing, God knows what. I was just hoping that my recently dyed beard hadn't started fading back to grey. We started talking and she kept feeding me free drinks. I had already had my share with Vreeland, but I happen to have a problem stopping once I start. Besides, the breakfast taco stand next door was open until midnight.

"I really miss going to the movies more than anything," she said.

"Me too. What's your favorite movie of all time?" I asked her.

"Hmmm. Probably one of the *Fast and the Furious* movies," she said. "The ones with Paul Walker."

I wasn't about to ask her if she had ever seen Chinatown.

I'm not sure what happened next, but after drink five, Casey began rubbing her legs against mine under the table.

'What the hell is happening?' I thought to myself. Here was a young girl, about 27, feeding me drinks and blatantly hitting on me. She asked me a peculiar question.

"Are you married?"

Oh boy. I crafted a clever answer.

"Not to anybody in Texas," I said.

"Come home with me," she answered.

I paused… this was weird. I had never cheated on my wife in our 15 years of marriage. I had never even been tempted, let alone hit on by a beautiful twenty-something cocktail waitress in a hotel lounge. I truly loved my wife, but what the hell had been happening to our relationship lately? I couldn't remember the last time we had had sex or kissed or even complimented each other. The couch sleeping was humiliating and I had overheard her talking to her friends recently about how she was pretty sure she wanted us to take some time apart. It didn't help that she spent most of her free time in the valley with her personal trainer and basically scoffed at every episode of a podcast I recorded, citing that she 'wasn't interested in true crime.'

Life had grown stale. And boring. Deep down, however, I was still convinced we had a chance to work things out.

I didn't think an opportunity like this would ever present itself, but it seemed dangerous and fun and I decided to take the flirtation a little further and see where it led me. I was an adventurous person after all - possibly in the middle of a mid-life crisis - and going to my hotel room to watch Netflix alone just didn't seem that appealing on my first night out on the town since the global pandemic shutdown was ordered.

I took a deep breath as I stared into her eyes...

"Why don't we just go to my room - I'm in room 25,'" I responded.

"No way," she replied. "I don't fuck where I work."

CHAPTER 2

A poster of Harry Styles stared down at me.

Casey tidied up her otherwise depressing south Austin apartment, picking up discarded wine bottles and laundry from the stained carpet. She tucked some stuff in her dresser and poured us wine from a nearby bottle that had probably been open for days. I was nervous, concerned and riddled with drunken anxiety. How was I in a 27-year-old girl's apartment? Was this a mistake? What would my wife say if she knew this was happening?

What the fuck are you looking at Harry Styles?

Casey took her top off in that weird one motion that women can do but men can't and then began to take her bra off. I paused. I wasn't sure I could go through with this.

"What about you?" She said.

"Uhm..."

"Oh come on, don't be scared... I know what I'm doing."

Casey inched closer to me and rubbed the side of my thigh. I immediately became aroused as I smelled her daisy-like breath drawing me into what could be an extra-marital affair. I wasn't sure what the hell to do. She began taking off my t-shirt.

I hoped she liked dad bods.

All kinds of thoughts raced through my mind. I thought of my wife. Our wedding day in wine country, the birth of our children, the moment I had proposed in Aspen... That youthful glow of our late 20's when we thought the world would fall into place like dominoes and that there was no possible way anything could come between us... Long before mortgages and kids and car payments and lost jobs and pandemics and parents aging and needing assistance... You know REAL LIFE SHIT.

I caught a reflection of us in her cheap floor length mirror that was balanced against the wall. I recognized it as the same Target mirror you can get at the store in the "A-Dormable" section for seven dollars. This place reminded me of all the Hollywood apartments I had been in with girls in my early 20's. Apartments that make you think there is no future for the cocktail waitresses and wannabe actresses of the world...

As Casey moved her lips in towards my neck all I could think about was roughly how long it would be before I would be joining my other divorced friends in a one-bedroom apartment in Koreatown. I wondered who was looking for a roommate.

I panicked.

"This is so bad. This is so bad..." I suddenly said. "I can't do this... I'm sorry."

"Why?" She said. "It's not like I'm going to brag to anybody that I had sex with you."

I wasn't sure if that was supposed to hurt my feelings, but it didn't. I couldn't think of anything else other than the looks of sadness on my family's faces if I took this any further.

"Sorry, this was a mistake," I said. "I can't believe it even went this far. Please don't tell anybody about this!"

Casey was done with me at this point. She had her t-shirt back on in about six seconds.

"You don't know what you're missing."

"I mean, I'm like, 100 percent serious," I pushed. "This never happened, I never came up here."

"I get it."

"Like, I may have to kill you to keep your mouth shut."

Oops. That comment wasn't meant to be serious at all, but it frightened her to the point where she ran to the bathroom, slammed the door and yelled at me through the cheap plywood.

"Get out!" She screamed. "Get the fuck out or I'll call the police!"

"I'm sorry, it was just a joke!"

"Get the fuck OUT!"

I gathered my clothes and got dressed. As I looked towards the way out, I quickly glanced down at an empty Sparkletts water bottle that was over-stuffed with cash. It struck me as being strange that this bartender who was living in basic squalor would have a Breaking Bad- like cash jar in her apartment, but I could only surmise that she had probably just been saving her tips from the bar. I pulled the door open and ran down stairs realizing that I had absolutely no idea where I was. Luckily my phone had 11 percent of a charge left - enough to order a Lyft back to the hotel. I felt like I was going to have a heart attack. I was in full blown panic mode. I paced in front of a liquor store that was about to close. I looked at my phone. My wife had called me three times. Fuck. This was the worst thing ever. I banged on the gate of the liquor store and said it was an emergency. The man, possibly reeling from a bad night himself, said he understood and I darted inside and bought American Spirit cigarettes with the only cash I had left. I hadn't smoked a cigarette in seven years. I smoked three in ten minutes waiting for my car.

Out of habit I overturned one of the cigarettes so that the filter faced upwards. Back in college this was known as "The LUCKY cigarette." You always saved it for last.

When my Lyft driver finally arrived, I jumped in and he raced me back through the empty streets to the Hotel San Joaquin. I jumped out, thanked him, smoked another cigarette and went to the taco stand. It was 2: 30 a. m. It was closed.

Defeated, I slowly inched back towards my room wondering if I had just lost a once-in-a-lifetime opportunity for a middle-aged man to feel young again for one night. I clumsily fumbled through my pockets looking for something but of course, it wasn't there.

I had lost that stupid room key.

CHAPTER 3

After paying $15. 00 for a new room key I finally got back into my room and noticed that somebody else had been there. I had left my laptop closed and on the bed, and now it was opened and on the counter. My bags had been rifled through but as far as I could tell, nothing had been taken. It was strange. I had been out of my room for roughly seven-and-a-half hours. What had transpired? I quickly checked the shower and thankfully found nobody there. I did notice, however, a strange shoe print that had been left in the bathroom. A smaller shoe print than mine (I wear a size 13) was clearly on the white linoleum tile. I took an iPhone photo of the tread pattern and went to see if anything was missing. At first glance, it didn't seem like anything was. Still, it was a violating feeling.

I tossed in bed most of the night, only catching small patches of sleep and having recurring nightmares about things like intruders, murderers, and home invasions. You know, the usual stuff true crime podcast producers dream about at night. It was like detoxing, but I had been properly oiled all evening. I'm pretty sure I was just feeling guilty about Casey. Top that off with the fact that I'm an anxiety-ridden Jew and it's amazing I made it through the night.

I almost wish I hadn't.

I wondered why things had been so strange since I had come to town. First, the experience with Casey. Did she lure me out of the hotel for a specific reason? So that someone could go into my room and search for something? What did I have to hide? I wasn't working on any true crime podcasts at that moment, so nobody would be out to stop my research. I once vomited into a fountain at a South by Southwest music festival that my old band was showcasing at - but that was in 2004. .. What had I done to this town? Also - Why had Alfie Adams reached out to me after 17 years? And who had been in my room?

Insomnia took me down a three hour Instagram wormhole and I took a look at Casey Dixon's account, noting her typical "Wannabe Influencer" pictures. Completely obnoxious and impossible to unsee. You know these Instagram girls? Some call them "Thirst Traps" or "Basic Bitches." As far as I could tell, Casey was one of those. She had roughly 18, 000 followers. Her last three posts were of her in a thong suntanning at Barton Springs Pool, Her in Yoga Pants holding up a "Black Lives Matter" sign in front of a boarded up bar off of 6th street downtown and her in a sexy one-piece bathing suit holding up two peace signs at the Hotel San Joaquin pool. She had numerous pictures of her and her "Betches" with their tongues out, at the Bonnaroo Festival and wearing impossibly short and shredded denim shorts that left very little to the imagination.

And then I got to her earliest posts.

Casey joined Instagram in 2012, when she was 19 and a junior at UT Austin. Her first post had been on campus while she was tailgating for a football game. She had on tight burnt orange shorts and a midriff shirt that said "Hook 'Em Horns." She was with a couple of sorority sisters and it was about as typical of a college girl post you could imagine. The caption read, "Sistahs for life, #Hookemhorns, #fuckedup, #Alphaphi #Drunkwknd." As I examined the photo a little deeper, I began to notice something familiar behind her and her sorority sister... In the background stood a lone man, looking as if he was stalking her, or at least very interested in her... I squinted as I took a closer look and wondered why he had seemed so recognizable when I first saw him... Then it hit me.

It was Alfie Adams.

CHAPTER 4

A deep internet search for Alfie Adams turned up a few strange things. For one, he had lived in Austin off and on from 2008-2014, and at one point apparently moved to Houston. His Linked In account showed his employer as a trucking company called "Horsepower" and listed his education as having graduated from UT Austin in 1998. Which is perplexing as to how he would show up in Casey's Instagram on-campus photo from 2012. He is listed as having no wife or children and has numerous references to his old band, Roadflowers, who had fizzled out after one mediocre album on Epic Records. In my opinion they only got signed because their lead singer looked like a Roman statue but I personally thought they were overrated and didn't deserve that record deal in the first place. But, back then, labels were signing acts with the intent to FAIL. It made sense when tax season came around.

My band was called Night Bears and we were a Southern California mix of cosmic and outlaw country music. We had a few minor label record deals and at one point placed a song in an episode of the TV show Franklin and Bash but otherwise we did that famed European club tour in 2003 and hung it up when all of us got married and became fathers. I wrote songs for a while, but eventually transitioned into the true crime podcast space, producing and writing over six series within the past 10 years that have brought six cold cases to justice. I was never interested in the true crime space per se, but once I solved my first case, I was hooked. I began producing my own materials and was hired to spearhead the true crime division of DETAIL, Inc. - a huge podcast company out of Los Angeles. We have deals with celebrities, chefs, hosts, actors, etc. and are sponsored and owned by a tech company called Crumb - so as long as we keep making content, the lights will stay on.

The Europe 2003 tour was, for me, the highlight of my music career. Even though we played to mostly empty places, we got to see the world on the record company's dime and we drank and partied across Europe for what I consider to be the last free summer of my youth.

Alfie Adams was the bass player in Roadflowers and we spent a lot of time in the same vans, hotel rooms and beer gardens hanging out. His real name was Allen Felix Adams, so "Alfie-Felix" somehow became "Al-Fee" and as I read about his band and listened to some of the old music, I recalled one memory of us both sort of competing over a girl named Marina or Gelina or something in Copenhagen. She spoke absolutely no English and as Alfie and I drank at her bodega, I started to notice that she was checking me out. Alfie noticed this too, and called "dibs" on her, as if she was a slice of pizza we were all picking out from a 24-hour kiosk.

"Are you serious?" I said. "You can't call 'dibs' - she has to decide between us."

I know this sounds crass in the year 2020, and as a middle-aged father with a daughter, I too recognize the shallowness and depravity of my adolescent self, but when you're in a touring band this is one way you make the hours pass by.

When Marina or Gelina got off work, she said one word to me in broken English:

"Walk?"

Alfie got angry and stormed out into the streets of Copenhagen and Marina or Gelina and I kissed against the side of a building. I distinctly remember Alfie cursing me out for stealing his girl. Marina or Gelina said something in her native language - which I detected as to mean "I have to go" and we parted ways and never saw each other again.

Alfie barely talked to me for the next three stops on the tour.

There is something eye-opening about kissing a girl who does not speak a word of English. It is a definite challenge to try to read somebody's body language rather than work off of verbal reactions. Of course, it can backfire too - as our bass player Scott discovered when a girl in Spain kept pointing at her stomach as they were walking down a beach. He just thought she was hungry. ...

Turns out, she was pregnant.

I wondered if Alfie had something to do with Casey taking me back to her apartment? I mean, it had all been so easy. I didn't even have to buy her dinner. After a long hotel shower and three cups of coffee from Momo's next door, I came to terms with my actions from the night before.

I was so happy I hadn't let it get any further. I felt good. Proud of myself. I finally mustered up enough courage to call my wife and luckily my daughter picked up her phone. I spoke to her and then to my son. When my wife got on, she seemed rattled, as if me leaving town had messed with something at the house. Our conversation was short and full of "Uh-huhs" and "Sounds greats" and as I hung up I felt a void between us that had seemed worse since I had landed in Austin.

I started to think that maybe I should have slept with Casey.

CHAPTER 5

Vreeland and I sat down in the commons of the university and I told him about the night before. About Casey and the strange Alfie emails. He told me he would look into Adams and see what his time at UT had been like. It's cool being friends with true crime enthusiasts because they'll do stuff like this for you.

"I don't know if I could have said 'no' to a half-naked girl," Vreeland admitted. "But I think you did the right thing."

"Yeah, I felt guilty for even going up there, but things are starting to clear up although my wife seemed weird when I called."

"Well, of course - you're drinking in Austin and she's stuck with the kids in LA home-schooling. Hey, when did you start smoking?"

I had been tapping the pack against my hand as he spoke. I took one out and lit it up.

"I quit seven years ago. I started again last night."

I lit the end of the American Spirit and exhaled into the Texas afternoon. A cigarette in 95 degree weather was not the brightest idea and I stubbed it out pretty quickly.

I had retrieved my rental car from Stereo earlier in the day and had breakfast tacos at a place on Yelp that had been described as "The most amazing breakfast taco you will ever have." To me it was a flour tortilla with cold eggs and cheese. The salsa was decent, but it wasn't enough to make me take a photo of the food and post to my social media account like everyone around me seemed to be doing.

On campus, which was practically empty, Vreeland relayed to me a new podcast pitch about legendary Texas country musician, one-time Gubernatorial candidate and mystery novelist Kinky Friedman and how one of his students had an 'in' with him for an interview. I nodded and said I'd like to see an overview of the project and then took a quick tour of his classroom and podcast recording spaces. It was all pretty boring, and we passed the time with chit-chat about gear and microphones and how great the recent podcast episodes of Most Notorious had been. Finally, I jumped on a Zoom call with a bunch of his students and spoke about the power of podcasting and bullshitted them into thinking that this existence was really more than internet searches and interviews. It was like the moment in Indiana Jones and the Last Crusade when he says "X never marks the spot."

"What about that podcast you did when you sent Vincent Caggiano to jail," one student asked. "You were in the field for, like, months on that one."

The student had been correct. The project was called The Cigarette Girl. That was an adventure that I barely came back from, having exonerated a wrongfully convicted man for the murder of a female casino employee in Las Vegas. The guilty man was an ex-gambler named Vincent Caggiano who had successfully framed his old business partner for the murder of a young cigarette girl from the Alladin Casino back in 2014. Amazingly, after a week in Vegas, I had sworn off booze for life, solved the crime and released my first multi-million download podcast.

That helped me get hired by DETAIL. I thanked the student for reminding me of my past accomplishments and we ended the call.

"Amazing. They pay all this tuition money to go to class from their apartments over Zoom," I said.

"Yeah, I wonder how long this model will hold up."

Vreeland and I decided to eat bar-be-cue out of town at the Salt House, a fairly popular and well known spot that locals still stand by even though foodies have moved onto smaller joints like Tejas and Terry Green's. I really hate bar-be-cue snobs, especially the ones who always have to gab on about some hidden BBQ shack in the back of a fucking East Austin gas station where they murder the animals in front of you before bathing them in sauce mixed with the blood of Pagans...

Just give me meat, beer, and sauce and get out of my way.

After eating half of a wild animal park and draining three beers, I decided a nap was in order. I said good-bye to Vreeland, drove back and pulled my rental car into the hotel parking lot.

Four Austin Police Department black and whites were now parked in the lot of the San Joaquin. I took a deep glance from my windshield and gathered the bottle of water I had purchased at a gas station down the street. I found my stupid little room key and made my way into the hotel. I avoided the lounge area and any chance of possibly running into Casey. It reminded me of taking different hallways to class in high school hoping to avoid some girl you had a crush on who turned down your prom invitation.

As I walked past the pool and noted the usual cocktail sippers swimming at 3:00 p.m., things began to close in around me. I felt like the entire hotel was staring me down and when I finally made it to my room, I dropped my bottled water to the ground as I opened my door.

Within seconds, I had been grabbed and thrown up against the wall, my hands tangled behind my back. A strong-armed police officer pushed handcuffs onto my wrist, and shouted the following:

"Robert Stoner... You are under arrest for the murder of Casey Dixon..."

CHAPTER 6

The Austin Police Department is cleaner than the Los Angeles Police Department. Not in a corrupt way, although I'm sure that statement holds true in that capacity as well. I was simply blown away by the sheer cleanliness of the facility. Like, it was a place where I'd consider having a wedding, or at the very least, my son's Bar Mitzvah.

A wide-shouldered sunburnt Latino police officer named Hernandez was staring me down with dark eyes and a no-nonsense scowl that reminded me of Christopher Meloni on episodes of Law and Order: SVU. A long time fan of that show, I had known that I had some rights to exercise here before I was just sent up the river for the murder of this poor young girl. First thought I had questions of my own. Why was I here? How was Casey killed? Are you sure she's even dead?

"How did it feel," Hernandez chirped.

"How did what feel?"

"How did it feel to kill her?"

"First of all, I'd like a lawyer. Secondly, I left her apartment last night at around 2:15."

"2:15 last night? Or 2:15 this morning?"

"What?"

"Was that after you killed her?"

"I didn't kill her! I basically went up there and went home."

"You think we're stupid?!" He yelled. "We have a witness!"

Shit man, what was happening here? I suddenly started panicking and called Vreeland. I asked him if he knew any lawyers... told him I was in some deep shit. He responded with a guy named Jefferson Tulack.

"Get me a Jew," I ordered. "I work better with Jews."

"Harder than you think in Texas."

According to the officers questioning me, Casey Dixon was strangled and left for dead in her apartment shortly after 3:00 in the morning. A neighbor described the man who had come back with her to her apartment and nailed my entire outfit to a t-shirt. The trucker hat, the Neil Young shirt and the "Attention Discount Shopper" white guy shorts. She even said I had on a "Neat blue fabric mask."

I now hate this fucking thing.

To top it all off, the neighbor claimed she heard me say one incriminating thing as I stood in Casey's apartment:

"Like, I may have to kill you to keep your mouth shut."

Fuck.

As I denied and denied every accusation, I was grilled about why there were cigarette butts outside of her apartment (Which were hand-rolled perfectly, not the American Spirits I was choking down), why there was a Spakletts bottle in Casey's apartment with over $3,000 cash stuffed in it and why I was still wearing a trucker hat for fashion at 45-years-old. (A sentiment my wife has also brought up in the past).

Sitting there patiently waiting for Vreeland to track down a lawyer, the detective kept turning the screws. Finally, he pulled out one piece of evidence that may just send your boy Robert Stoner up the highway and over to join the Texas Prison Rodeo.

They had found the dumb hotel keychain I had left in Casey's apartment.

Room 25.

CHAPTER 7

I was told that my room at the Hotel San Joaquin had been scrubbed clean and that they were looking for evidence of any involvement with Casey Dixon on my end. My luggage and backpack and laptop had all been confiscated and they were going through that stuff as well. I explained that I had come home after turning down Casey's advances and found that my room had been rifled through and that I had a photo of a shoe imprint on the bathroom floor. I showed the detectives that photo on my iPhone and they promptly confiscated my iPhone.

"Doesn't the Hotel San Joaquin have security cameras?" I asked.

"We're looking into that."

"What about Casey's apartment building? I mean, it's 2020 - I have a God Damn private fortress-level Ring camera set up at my own house in L.A."

"Checking that as well. You sure ask a lot of questions for a murder suspect."

"Look," I said. "I produce and write true crime podcasts for a living. I have solved six cold-case murders. You're not turning over the right rocks here... and you've got the wrong guy."

Just then, as I leaned back and ran my hands through my thinning hair wondering if I was about to spend the rest of my life with a prison roommate learning how to make "toilet merlot," a female detective named Suarez walked in the room holding my laptop.

"We got him," she said. "It appears that Mr. Stoner sent an email admitting he was planning on killing her around 11 PM last night."

"What?"

"Sorry, pal. Looks like Travis State Jail for you."

"I was at the hotel bar at 11 PM! Nowhere near my laptop!"

"Then surely you can show us a receipt for your purchases."

Shit. I recalled that Casey had been floating me drinks all night. My only charge was for the glass of $14.00 Rioja I had purchased around 7 before I hooked up with Vreeland.

Which made me wonder if Casey was giving me free drinks so that there would BE no evidence...

But now she was dead so that made no fucking sense. Unless someone had set her to do this to me so that they could gain access to my room.

What the hell had happened after I had left her apartment? At this point, only the killer and Harry Styles knew. I guess there are less attractive men you'd want on your wall watching you as you take your last breath.

As the detectives gathered around my laptop in the other room, I began weeping. I was always a tremendous pussy, admittedly so, and now I was facing 25 to life for some weird shit that was impossible to tiptoe around. I wouldn't last one day in prison. Unless there was some hard core Jewish gang I could join, I was set to get raped, wrung up, and shanked twenty minutes after settling into my jail cell. I was lost. What email could I have sent at 11 o'clock? I was drinking with Casey at that time in the hotel lounge. It had to be on the hotel video somewhere. Don't they have a fucking RING camera?

Just then, as I felt that all hope was about to be lost, a man named Robert Mandelbaum walked in.

"Rob? I'm Rob. I'm your lawyer, Rob Mandelbaum. Friend of Vreeland's."

"Thank God man! They're, like, ready to put me on Death Row."

"Let's start from the beginning."

I told Mandelbaum everything. About Alfie Adams, Casey and how I had a moment of weakness before spurning her advances, the weird feeling that someone had been in my hotel room, the footprint… He took it all in and told me one thing I didn't need to hear.

"You probably shouldn't have gone to her apartment in the first place."

"Yeah, no shit."

"And did you really threaten to kill her?"

"That was a joke… A really stupid fucking horrible joke."

Mandelbaum was what author Rich Cohen would have called a "Tough Jew" in his recent book about, well… tough Jews. He was a fighter and a big, bruiser-like presence. He was like a few of my Jewish fraternity brothers I knew at UC Santa Barbara who had parents in the Mossad and could drink and fight anti-Semitic parasites from the central coast who would come down to our parties and draw Swastikas on our fraternity house doors. Being in a Jewish fraternity didn't guarantee you would get laid, but it did guarantee that when you needed a loan from a fraternity brother ten years down the road, he would probably be there for you.

Or act as your lawyer.

Robert Mandelbaum had grown up in Cherry Hill, New Jersey, across from Philadelphia. He wanted nothing more than to get away from the East Coast winters so he trekked across the country to UT Austin in 1996 where he spent his undergrad years taking mushrooms and touring around the country in a van following the band Phish before settling into a respectable life as a criminal defense lawyer. He had recently defended a man accused of rustling cattle outside of Austin.

"Wait, cattle rustling is still a thing?"

"You betcha."

As the detectives came back in to question us some more, I felt better that Mandelbaum was there to help. They took out my laptop and opened my email account. They opened up the 'Sent' folder and showed Mandelbaum and myself an email I apparently had sent at 11:01 PM the night before. It read:

I can't live with this anymore. It's too much and I can never face my family with my secret. After I kill Casey, I'm killing myself.

The email was addressed to an anonymous tip email hotline at the Austin Police Department and blind copied to an email address that I wasn't able to see. The police were able to uncover it using their tech experts... It was sent to someone named Tony Valero.

CHAPTER 8

I spent the night in the police station repeating my story. I think their plan was to break me or force me into some sort of confession but I was repeating the same details over and over. The questions they kept asking were not making me comfortable.

"So, you like having one-night stands with cocktail waitresses?"

"You were going to kill yourself, huh? How many times have you been unfaithful to your wife?"

"Why are you here in Texas?"

As they went down every rabbit hole, I felt like there was no way out of this scenario. It didn't help that Vreeland had to report to my boss back in Los Angeles what was going on. I was pretty sure I was going to be fired for this and was just counting the hours.

The walls were closing in around me.

"The good news, Mr. Stoner?" Hernandez barked. "Is that due to this Covid-19 shit, all 'in-person visitation rights' are suspended at Travis State Prison, so you probably won't be able to see your wife and kids... like ever again."

I took a deep breath just as a third detective came in with more unsettling news.

"All the security cameras at Hotel San Joaquin were disabled last night. Staff says only people who worked there would know how to do it."

"So we have no footage of Mr. Stoner entering the facilities last night?"

"All we have is him leaving his room at around 11:30 this morning."

"What about the footprint in the bathroom?" I offered.

Mandelbaum shushed me. He had been staying back, preparing a killer strike that would eventually get me out of that station and out to the 95 degree freedom I was so desperately craving.

"Detectives, please open my client's iPhone Lyft app and check his recent ride history."

Oh shit. The Lyft!

I started thanking God for that 11% charge that had been just enough to get me a ride. Sure enough, there it was. On my phone... A ride with Rorthap, a Turkish driver who had picked me up in front of the liquor store beneath Casey's apartment at about 2:17 AM and dropped me back at the Hotel San Joaquin at 2:30 AM. The detectives reported that the murder took place around 3:00 in the morning, according to an neighbor witness who heard an aggressive struggle and called the police.

Holy shit, I was free.

Rorthap even gave me a five-star rating.

"Detectives - my client can no longer be held here without definitive concrete evidence. If you have a murder weapon or DNA evidence or video footage you may keep him, but until that happens, an email that he never sent and the proof of his Lyft ride is not enough to hold him at this time."

There was a deafening silence in the room.

"He's right," Suarez said, walking back in. "The rape kit came back negative. Doesn't look like Ms. Dixon was sexually assaulted or had intercourse within the past 24 hours…"

"He could have used a condom," Hernandez said.

"The latex would have shown up in the kit. Here's the other news: Casey Dixon was two months pregnant."

The detectives stared at each other for a while in silence, eventually mumbling to each other how saddened they were finding out that there was a baby involved.

They then turned their gaze back to myself and Mandelbaum.

"Mr. Stoner, you are free to go."

The air came back into the room. Wildlife began perking up and started swaying in the breeze like those nature videos we used to watch in science class where they filmed a time lapse of blooming plants and sunrises and caterpillars turning into butterflies.

After nine hours of questioning, I was set free. But not without a warning and an ominous truth that even I couldn't deny.

"Mr. Stoner this is an active investigation and you are currently a potential murder suspect in this case. You are not allowed to leave the city of Austin or the state."

Shit. More Texas.

CHAPTER 9

I had 81 missed texts and phone calls. My wife had been reaching out, asking me where I was. I wasn't sure how to tell her that I was currently a suspect in a murder investigation that took place after I followed a 27-year-old girl to her tiny apartment. My laptop would remain in police custody until they could search all my internet history. I panicked thinking about my search history and prayed to God that the XXX websites I had visited during a "Private Window Session" a day earlier on the couch at home had really been erased from the computer's IP.

Mandelbaum drove me out of the station and we made our way back to the south Congress area so I could gather my stuff and check out of that hotel before the staff started calling me a murderer and throwing wet tacos at me.

"How'd you know about my Lyft ride?" I asked. "I didn't even think about that."

"I drive Lyft on the side. I can't tell you how many times I've used this app as a way out for accused criminals."

"But... you're a lawyer. Why drive Lyft?"

"People confess some serious shit to Lyft drivers, man. It's like free therapy. I can read anybody."

I snuck through the side entrance of the Hotel San Joaquin and slid over to room 25 and noticed that it had been sealed off with Police Line Do Not Cross tape. I went to the front desk and attempted to check out. The young lady working there was in tears and whispering about Casey with her co-worker as she presented me with my receipt - which was $750 for two nights - and my luggage from the room. I took one last look at the lounge and realized that I would probably never set foot in this hotel ever again. It's weird when you go through something like this...You have to be prepared to never be able to set foot in certain places again.

It was 6:45 in the morning and I was starving.

"Too early for bar-be-cue?" I asked Mandelbaum.

"Not in Texas."

Twenty minutes later we pulled into a back of a gas station BBQ spot I had never heard of called "Shank." Fitting, I thought for my near prison experience. Mandelbaum told me it was the best hidden backwoods Bar-be-cue in town and I was so hungry I didn't care. I ordered pork ribs and brisket at 7 in the morning and devoured the entire thing with two beers. Healthy breakfast, but I suddenly came back alive.

"What do you think happened," Mandelbaum asked me after I mowed through the meat without stopping to breathe. "Who killed her?"

"I don't know," I said feeling my facial tissues slowly swell up due to excessive salt. I pulled off of the Lone Star Beer and thanked Mandelbaum for his help.

"No problem man. I gotta tell you, when I first heard this story, I thought you were guilty as hell."

"Really? I've never hurt a fly."

"Well, someone obviously set you up to make it look like you were behind this. I mean, the email, the video cameras... something weird was going down at the Hotel San Joaquin and if I were you I'd look into the folks working there."

"Man, this is just like my podcast Prairie Killer, I said. "I was able to exonerate a guy locked up for murder by tracking down iPhone towers and receipts from a hotel."

"Well, I'm just a lawyer or else I'd help you out... but maybe you are your next project."

"Hmm," I thought. "Not a bad idea. I just never thought I would ever be the guy who was being set up to be taken down."

Following breakfast, I went downtown to get a much cheaper room in a less hip location. I found a La Quince Inn for $119 and took the elevator as quickly as I could to avoid any interaction with other guests. This was a pandemic after all and I had originally chosen the Hotel San Joaquin because of its outdoor distancing and lack of elevators. The La Quince Inn was the exact opposite.

Downstairs in the breakfast area, which had been shuttered due to the pandemic, middle class families with dads wearing socks inside sandals prepared to cover the town as tourists and see God-knows-what. Austin is a cool town, but not exactly one where you take the kids on vacation. Unless they have a particular interest in Stevie Ray Vaughn statues and tacos.

I was exhausted and went upstairs to my room, which I paid an extra 25 dollars for to guarantee an early check in. I hit the bed and only woke up five hours later because my phone hadn't stopped ringing the entire time.

"Jesus Christ," I said, rolling over and finally seeing who couldn't lay off of my phone number. The caller ID said "Vreeland."

"Hey man, sorry I should have called you earlier," I groaned into the phone.

"I spoke with Mandelbaum... he thinks you're really lucky that you had that Lyft record or else you'd be on your way out to Travis State."

"Yeah man, something sinister is happening here."

"Well, yeah - it is. Remember how I said I'd do some research on Alfie Adams' time at the university?"

"Yeah?"

"I found a treasure trove. This guy was a total scumbag... where can we meet?"

I drove the rental back over towards south Congress, stopping only when I noticed a newspaper on a newsstand reporting the death of Casey Dixon. I decided to grab a copy and read it over the first chance I got. I moved slowly up the street to meet Vreeland, noticing that for Austin, this place was pretty deserted. This pandemic had kept everybody indoors. The good news was you could dart in and out of traffic and not have to waste too much time pumping the brake pedal. The bad news was that I had noticed two squad cars tailing me about 75 yards back.

I played a few games, stopping twice to see if they stopped as well. They did, but half a street back. If this was supposed to be a clandestine operation, it was not going well and these guys could have been the worst hide-in-plain-sight cops I had ever seen, It was almost comical when I pulled into the North Congress Cafe to meet Vreeland and they passed by and parked half a block up.

Vreeland was on the back patio where the fans were blowing the mister air all around, spreading Covid-19 amongst all over the customers but at a much more effective rate. He had a Bloody Mary going and one awaiting me as well.

"Best in town," he said.

I sipped the drink, even though I didn't necessarily want it, and noted that it actually was really damn good. I sat down by Vreeland and told him that I had left the Hotel San Joaquin and was now holed up in the La Quince, where the bottles of wine in the mini bar were a lot more affordable than the glasses of wine at the San Joaquin. Even though, I guess, I didn't pay for the wine at the San Joaquin.

It hit me again that Casey and her unborn child were dead. I slammed the rest of the Bloody Mary and asked Vreeland what he could show me.

"OK, this guy Adams went to UT Austin for two years, never graduated."

"It says he graduated on his Linked In page," I responded.

"Yeah? It says my sister is a doctor on her Linked In page. She's a wet nurse in Laredo."

"What about Adams? What do we have?"

"OK, never graduated, but hung around campus for a long time. Like, a LONG time. Three complaints about him stalking young women around campus, one dropped sexual assault charge. He used to get drunk at tailgate parties and hit on these young girls even when he was well into his 30's."

"Jesus."

"And get this. At one point, he had a flier up on campus trying to recruit members for a rock band. The flier said, Sex, Drugs, Rock-n-Roll! Former signed bass player is looking for a drummer, guitarist and lead singer to rock! Influences: Rage Against the Machine, Uncle Tupelo and Tesla.

"Tesla?"

"Yep. Then it says, Join a band, get bitches! This guy was a grade A creep. Campus security had to remove the fliers and he was permanently banned from campus around 2017."

"Funny, Casey went to UT in 2012. I wonder if they ever met."

"Well, does this answer your question?"

Vreeland handed me a manila envelope. I wasn't sure what I was expecting to see inside, but it was labeled "Dixon Complaint Against Adams, A. 2013."

Inside were a few papers and a photo of a man I only half-recognized as Alfie Adams. In 2003 he had cool, shaggy hair and was skinny as a rail. In this photo, it looked as if time had caught up with him pretty hard. His hair was stringy and he looked puffy and bloated. One of them looked like a mugshot, but was simply a photo of him on a grainy security camera.

it turns out that Dixon had issued a restraining order against Adams and had claimed she caught him pleasuring himself outside of her apartment during her sophomore year. Apparently, Adams left her love notes on her car and was obsessed with her. At one point, according to the documents, Casey had gone back to Dripping Springs, where she was from, and he started showing up.

"Austin police have records of the restraining order too, but this was the complaint she filed with campus police," Vreeland said.

As I sat back and wondered if I should have a second Bloody Mary, my mind started swirling with possibilities of what the hell was actually happening. Suddenly, my iPhone alerted me that I had a new email. I acutely became aware that it had been two days since I had spoken to my wife and kids. I opened the email and Vreeland watched as my face fell.

I had just been fired.

CHAPTER 10

The last time I was fired from a job was in 1992. I had landed a gig that year as a busboy at the local Tucson, Arizona 50's-themed diner "Little Archie's" and I spent three weeks clearing plates and pocketing cash tips meant for waiters and dancing around to Run-around Sue.

All of the employees had fake "50's-style" names. Dion, Georgie, Fonzie. Somehow, I drew the name Putzie.

When the diner manager demanded that Putzie go clean puke out of the bathroom stall, I lost it. I realized I had bigger and better things on the horizon and I promptly told him to fuck off.

I was fired on the spot.

Until I was accused of murder, that was the only time I was ever fired from a job.

Turns out Casey Dixon had been fired from FIVE jobs.

Even though she was in her mid 20's, the young lady had been let go at two previous hotels, including the sister hipster hotel up the street called the Armadillo. According to files Vreeland found for me in the UT archives, Casey had been caught sneaking into renters' rooms when the folks were out. Sound familiar? When guests complained about the missing cash in their room or how their bags looked tampered with, the hotel manager chalked it up to the cleaning service. As it turns out, Ms. Dixon was doing some cleaning of her own...

Looks like I had to go back to the Hotel San Joaquin for some answers.

I was able to track down Casey Dixon's past employment history from the manager at the San Joaquin, a friendly guy named Mike Porter who wore jeans, a $500 flat-brimmed hat and a long-sleeved shirt even in 75 percent humidity. There was a time in my life when fashion trumped comfort when I was around Mike's age, and be it 100 degrees or not, I would force myself into cowboy boots, jewelry and stage-worthy snap shirts to uphold some weird rock-n-roll cosmic cowboy image I had created for myself... But then I got older and re-discovered the brilliant world of basketball shorts, flip flops and t-shirts.

In 2020 alone, I believe I had worn jeans exactly twice.

Mike Porter showed me Casey's job application. She was a UT graduate, had worked at a restaurant, a vape store, a hotel in her hometown, the Armadillo Hotel and an overpriced thrift store called "The Sundown." Under reason for dismissal, she had jotted down, "Left on my own accord." Mike recalled hiring her.

"Yeah, I called a few places for references. Most of the time the people I reached from her old jobs didn't sound too angry about her dismissal."

"Wait," a voice called out from behind the back desk.

When you hear the word 'wait' coming from anybody, you hope that they are about to give you some interesting news, or that they are answering a question about something that you gained over the holidays.

Of course, that version is spelled "weight."

"Wait," the assistant manager, a friendly girl named Laura who was listening in to our conversation said again. "I remember that there was something weird about the thrift store…"

"Please, continue."

'I don't remember that - " Mike said.

"Yes you do!" Laura rattled off.

I had to end this lovers' quarrel quickly.

"Hey, Mike? Will you please let Laura speak for a second?"

Mike nodded and hid his face in his overpriced flat-brimmed hat.

"Casey had given us the phone number of her former boss," Laura said. "I called this guy and he said that Casey had left after three months and that she said she wanted to get back into the hospitality profession…here's the thing - I know other folks who work at the Sundown thrift store. They remembered Casey, but none of them remembered the name of the guy she had me call for a reference for her."

"What was his name?" I asked.

"Tony Valero."

The name seemed familiar. And then I remembered… According to the Austin PD, I had apparently emailed a guy named "Tony Valero" claiming that I was a guilt-ridden, sex-obsessed psycho suicidal killer at 11:01 PM the night Casey died.

These coincidences were starting to add up faster than a bachelorette party bar bill down on 6th Street.

"So, wait - you still hired her even though that was an obvious lie?"

Michael jumped back in.

"To tell you the truth, from what I remember, I didn't care. I was in need of a server, she was gorgeous and she brought in more money for our lounge than anybody who has ever worked here."

"What about the stolen property people had reported from the Hotel Armadillo?"

"She claimed it was some misunderstanding."

"So who could have disconnected the security cameras?" I asked.

"All employees have access to the code. It shuts off the cameras, WiFi, basically anything technological."

"I need a list of all employees who had a link to this code."

"Sure."

As Mike printed out a list of employees with the codes, I glanced down at the hotel merchandise table. Over a dozen different soft t-shirts reading "Hotel San Joaquin" were for sale with southwestern themes and wine keys, beer coozies, bandanas... it was like I was at a concert watching people shell out hundreds of dollars for silk-screened graphic t-shirt with Blake Shelton's dimpled face on it.

"Noticing our merch, huh?" Mike said. "I'll give you 15 percent off on anything."

"I'll pass."

I went back to the La Quince Hotel and decided to start calling employees under a fake name. I occasionally dropped re-enactment voices into my true crime podcasts and was getting pretty good at disguising my voice. I was growing especially good at southern characters and figured that if I could get some Hotel San Joaquin employees to talk, I may be able to get some information. The first name on the list was Ruby Anderson.

"Hello?"

"Hi, Ms. Anderson - this is Detective Nick Sproles from the Austin Police Department. I'd like to ask you some questions regarding Casey Dixon."

Ruby seemed terrified and scared. I couldn't blame her. It made sense. A young woman - who she happened to have worked with - was dead.

"I just heard. So scary... do you guys have any idea who did it?" She said.

"Not yet, ma'am. Just wondering if you knew her or an acquaintance named Tony Valero."

"No. Never heard of him."

We hung up. As I went down the list, I must have reached out to 15 more employees only to have NONE of them answer their phones. Only Ruby had picked up, and she was my first call... I get it, I hate talking on the phone too.

I decided to pause on cold-calling employees and check out the Sundown Thrift Store.

The Sundown had been an Austin staple since the days when Janis Joplin was shopping there for gypsy leathers and feathered boas in the mid 1960's. It had recently gone under a bit of a makeover, catering more towards kids looking for vintage Air Jordan's and Champion basketball jerseys than for tie-dyed Grateful Dead shirts, but it still had an Austin feel. The bell-bottoms and cowboy boots, hats and t-shirts were all big sellers in town and as I walked through their dusty racks, I found myself picking out items for myself. An Old 97's band tour t-shirt, a feathered Urban Cowboy-era cowboy hat and one of Willie Nelson's joke books. As I brought it to the young lady working the cash register, I felt as if I was back to those pre-flip flops and basketball shorts days when my stage outfits defined me.

I walked up to the register and met Ryann, a lovely 30-something hippie cowgirl wearing a David Allen Coe t-shirt. Townes Van Zandt songs echoed over the store stereo and it reminded me of what my old banjo player Jim Dragster Kalin used to tell me:

"Never trust anyone who can't play Pancho and Lefty on guitar."

I bought the three items for about 40 bucks and asked Ryann if she had ever met with or worked with Casey Dixon. I showed her Casey's Instagram page and Ryann took a while before recognizing her... She them told me one rather insane fact:

"Oh yeah, she was that methy chick who worked here for a few weeks right when I started, but then she left."

Wait, what? "Methy chick?" Something here was strange. Casey was definitely skinny, but in no way did she look like a girl addicted to methamphetamines. She had above average teeth and a bubbly personality, but if someone told me she was addicted to crystal meth,

I would have never believed them. Even her apartment showed no signs of drug abuse. Unless that Sparkletts bottle of cash was drug money? She didn't seem like a meth dealer. But then again, isn't that what all functioning addicts and dealers do? Hide their evidence? I thought back to the time when I hid cigarettes from myself as a way to avoid that drunken temptation to start again about 8 years ago. Of course, after ransacking the house looking for them, I realized that I had to quit...

By the way, I found them in the top tank of our toilet about a year ago. I nearly destroyed our septic system.

If Casey Dixon was a meth addict, Tony Valero was a real person and Alfie Adams was somehow a middle man, I suddenly began thinking that I was already in way over my head. I had a few leads, some phone numbers and I was still legally supposed to stay in Austin until I was 100 percent cleared of any wrongdoing. To top that off, I still needed to tell my wife about everything and get back to L. A. to somehow beg for my job back. In fact, I hadn't even spoken to my boss since he had fired me...

But I had an idea.

I was now a massive leading character in a murder mystery. I had been framed, falsely accused and given new information that might blow the doors off of a massive conspiracy involving thrift stores, hipster hotels, meth dealers and murder. I'm not sure why it took me this long to realize this, but I was suddenly hit with a Texas flood of clarity.

I went back to the hotel and began recording episode one of a new, active true crime podcast into my phone recorder...

It was called Austin Translation.

CHAPTER 11

Back at the hotel, the front desk delivered me a package that I desperately needed. My laptop from the Austin Police. Inside was a note of apology and two free pencils. I finally called my wife. My daughter answered again, asking if I was still coming home that night. I told her I couldn't, asked for my wife and broke down what was happening. Sort of.

"Look. I have to stay here, I'm a witness to a murder and I may have to testify about something."

"WHAT?" She screamed in my ear.

"A girl at the hotel I stay at was murdered. I was one of the last people to see her alive - look, it's complicated and I want to come home and oh, by the way... I lost my job."

"You're kidding."

"No. This is just bad press for them so they had to let me go."

"I don't believe you."

"Really? Well, YOU try to call the Austin Police Department and find me a way to get back to L.A. I'm not even allowed to leave Austin!"

She hung up on me. I called her back. This time my son answered.

"Where's mom?" I asked.

"She went to see her trainer. Paul."

"Wait, Paul? How do you know her trainer's name?"

My son paused his video game and took a deep breath.

"Why wouldn't I know his name? He was here for dinner last night."

CHAPTER 12

I spent the night looking at my Ring app on my iPhone.

Sure enough, the night before, Paul, a ripped, 6'5" specimen with shoulders that looked like snap-on pieces of one of my son's old superhero action figures came over around 4:30 p.m. I watched as he sauntered into my house like a cowboy heading into a saloon to claim his "soiled dove." Oh, and he was wearing NO mask by the way. Now, we don't really have any workout room or even a comfortable place to stretch in our house, so I figured that he was there for a peculiarly early dinner... but, dinner at 4:30? I kept watching the Ring. The most messed up thing about being 2000 miles away and watching recorded activity over your iPhone is that all secrecy and discretion in this world is now gone. Ever watch Mad Men? In today's world, Don Draper would have been divorced and homeless by now had technology been where it is today.

Our other home Ring camera is set up on the side of the house, where the cars are parked, When Paul rolled up in his 2020 Range Rover SUV and parked behind my 2013 Nissan Leaf electric, I could practically feel my penis crawling up inside my body. Paul had a Yoga mat with him, a leather fanny pack and he was sporting a t-shirt with an image of the band Hall and Oates wearing aerobics gear that read "SQUAT ROCK."

According to my Ring app, Paul did indeed stay for dinner. He most likely stayed for dessert as well as his car didn't pull out of the driveway until well after 11 o'clock at night. I was beginning to think that my days in my house were coming to a close... and it only added to the anxiety and heartbreak I was dealing with out here.

To take my mind off of my wife's possible indiscretions, I retreated downstairs for a few cigarettes before recording an opening to this new true crime podcast idea into my Garage Band and Blue Snowball microphone. I basically read the facts of the case, told the story about the police detectives arresting me and started setting up cliffhangers for each episode, Never one to outline an entire series, I figured I'd just get the basics down and see how it went from there. After all, if I had really lost my job, I was gonna have to start another one fairly quickly... and luckily podcasting is something you can do by yourself if you have the skill set. This job just wouldn't have any health or travel perks. At least for a while anyway.

After recording, I was exhausted and drank two mini wine bottles from my La Quince fridge and went to bed. That night, I dreamt... or recalled some other fond memories from that fateful Europe 2003 tour.

After France, Alfie Adams had started rolling his own cigarettes the entire time. On trains, street corners and in bus depots, we would always look forward to an "Alfie roll" because he had the most precise technique and I liked that about him, since I was perennially bumming them from him and re-paying him with beers at hostels and hotels. We were both keeping fastidious journals or our travels at the time, assuming that someday we would come back to read them and smile and keep our minds sharp with the youthful throwbacks of our mid 20's. All of my journals had been lost in some move years ago... What I remembered though, were Alfie's custom rolled cigarettes and how easy it was for us to talk to girls by showing off his tobacco and paper prowess.

I believe it was in Amsterdam when we decided to take mushrooms and go to the park. It was a lovely day full of cartoonish clouds and frisbees and dogs who wanted to play with you and endless laughter. Alfie had rolled 20 cigarettes and about 5 joints for the trip and I watched as he held court amongst the down-and-out hippie girls we had met earlier in the afternoon at the Grasshopper Cafe. I recalled that one of them had spent her entire summer collecting colorful plastic forks that they gave you in Europe to eat French Fries with at McDonald's. Anyway, on drugs, Alfie always seemed to be in control. It was when he was off of them that shit often went sideways... For instance, he would just take off into the streets after coming down. We never knew where he went, but he would always end up back at the youth hostel a few hours later. I was always somewhat even-keeled while taking drugs, even though I would occasionally get super paranoid and insecure. It took me a few years after quitting smoking weed to recognize that I was actually a pretty prolific and creative person without the stimulants and by the time I was in my 30's, I had sworn off drugs forever.

Alfie not so much. I woke up fairly early the next morning and decided to write him back from my email.

Dear Alfie, wow! Long time no see... Sorry it's taken me a few days to get back to you, but oh man - how are you? How did you know I was in Austin? Instagram, right? Dude - lots to catch up on - I'm here for a few days... Oh, and do remember our old friend Tony Valero? I ran into him yesterday! Small world, huh? - cheers brother - Stoner.

OK. So I was playing some cards. If Alfie and Tony Valero were somehow connected, I would be a genius. If he didn't respond, I would forget it... but something was strange. I Googled Tony Valero's in Austin and could only find a guy in San Antonio with the same name who built tiny houses. Either Tony Valero didn't exist, or he was dealing meth out of a tiny house just off of the Riverwalk.

I called the number I found online.

"Valero Construction. This is Miguel."

"Hi Miguel, I am looking for Tony Valero."

"Is this a joke?"

"No, why –" and then catching myself. "I would like to speak to Mr. Valero."

"Señor, Mr. Valero's been dead for 20 years."

CHAPTER 13

I met Vreeland at an off-campus bar for a podcast discussion. I needed help. This was all too much. Cops trailing me, a dead cocktail waitress, dead Valeros, dead marriages... I needed an intern.

"Can you find me someone from your program who can help me?" I pleaded.

"Well, bad news is, Rob - we don't really work together anymore, ya know? I'm sorry you got let go, but I have to mind my business as well - I can't have my department brought down because you were a suspect in a murder."

"I know, man - I know. But look - I'm working on this case as a project now! I'm going to be the first person arrested for murder to find the real killer during a true crime podcast!"

Vreeland nodded his head. I could see his mind racing. He exhaled sharply and looked around the outdoor picnic tables.

"Look, your idea to solve this case is fascinating, but I can't have UT involved. But, I may be able to get you some help."

"Go on."

"Lindsay Wi is an associate professor who works part-time with us. Sometimes she helps out our students with research for their shows and she loves your podcasts and may be able to help a little, but at this time, I'm out Rob. I'm sorry."

Losing Vreeland was a big hit, but I understood. If he was working with me and my old boss found out, Vreeland's entire podcast network could be shuttered. I agreed to meet with Lindsay and Vreeland graciously gave me her phone number. I texted her immediately and she responded a few minutes later.

I said good-bye to Vreeland, for now, and made my way to meet Lindsay on her lunch hour at a food truck called Sogo Japanese. The line was long. Especially for what they were serving.

"Japanese food from a truck in Texas?" I said to nobody in particular.

"This place is the best, man - best chicken and rice and fish cake anywhere," a student six feet in front of me replied.

As I mulled over the fact that we were thousands of miles away from Japanese waters, the seafood truck reminded me of an all-you-can-eat sushi buffet in Las Vegas that once gave me food poisoning. I also recalled an article the LA Weekly put out a few years ago exposing sushi restaurants for conning customers into believing tilapia was really yellowtail sashimi. Buy cheaper fish, put some food coloring in it... up charge the naive. It's not a joke. Fraudulent sushi crime is real. After all, how many patrons are going to take the time to examine the fish they're eating after three Sake's and a tall Sapporo?

"Robert?" Said a tender voice from behind me.

"You must be Lindsay."

Lindsay was wearing a long blouse over jeans, with a backpack slung over her shoulder. She was older than the students, possibly in her late 20's, and she was of Asian descent. She smiled as she elbow bumped me.

"Wow, I am such a fan of your work," she exclaimed. The Lake Jenny podcast was amazing. I had no idea you could track somebody's actions based on mating activities of wild animals."

That was a long story. I had the Jackson Hole National Park Rangers to thank for that one.

"Yeah, in reality most killers just don't think about what evidence they're leaving behind," I said. The same could have been said about The Cigarette Girl podcast - that was the one that broke my podcast cherry in overlooking evidence. It was also my biggest success.

Lindsay took her mask down and stared at the food truck.

"Hey, you should try the yellowtail roll here. It's so good."

I passed on the food truck sushi, but Lindsay seemed to enjoy hers and as we sat eating, I sort of regretted the crappy falafel I ordered from another food truck up the way. I filled her in on some information regarding the case and she seemed extremely excited to help me - which was a pleasant surprise.

Lindsay Wi was a Korean-American from Orange County, California. She had attended UC Irvine with intentions of becoming a lawyer before switching to journalism and writing columns for the Orange County Register about the plights of Korean War orphans living in America 50 years after the fact. Her stories were interesting and earned her high praise as a writer and when UT Austin came calling, she was summoned to join the staff as an associate professor just a few years back.

"Let's start with some names," I said. "Ever hear of a guy named Alfie Adams?"

"Only in those files that Vreeland gave you."

"What about Casey Dixon?"

"The murdered girl? I wasn't aware of her until the story in the paper a couple of days ago. I know her parents were here cleaning out her apartment last week. It was really sad."

I couldn't imagine the horror that those poor parents were going through. It made me want to solve this crime even more.

"OK, finally, what about the name Tony Valero?"

"I've heard of a guy named Anthony Valero."

"What? Who is he? What does he do?"

Lindsay tapped through her phone until she had come up with a website that she shared with me for a winery in Texas Hill Country called Longhorn Creek Estates. The heading of the page read as follows:

At Longhorn Creek Estates we blend the choicest grapes with our family knowledge of regions, climate and flavor to create a one-in-a-million like wine experience born deep in the heart of Texas... Our owner Anthony Valero brought his Italian family knowledge of grapes and harvesting to Hill Country nearly 20 years ago and has won numerous awards for his red blends, Malbec and chilled Rose'. Tasting available outside for small parties with reservations only.

As I looked through the web pages and examined all the available options, I marveled at something that had escaped my knowledge for the past 45 years of my life. It made me question all that I thought I had known as a worldly man with half a lifetime's experience behind him. And I shook my head in disbelief, I repeated the same thing quietly inside my head.

Texas has a wine country?

CHAPTER 14

I had a message waiting for me at the La Quince Inn from Detective Hernandez at the Austin Police Department.

I called him from my hotel phone.

"Mr. Stoner. You're free to leave Texas. We arrested someone for Casey's murder last night."

"What? Who?"

"Building superintendent. Real sick fucker. Had Casey's underwear and the murder weapon in his apartment - had been stalking her for years."

"Holy shit."

"So, look. Huge apologies for the misunderstanding - we were just following leads and doing our jobs. You understand, right?"

I understood. But I wasn't sure how I felt about this. I was knee deep into a podcast about the Casey Dixon murder. I had no idea how Alfie Adams or Tony Valero were involved, but somehow, somewhere the police were missing some key clues on this case. A superintendent? It seemed too easy. Was this case closed? Worst thing was, I had just dedicated myself to solving this crime via a podcast and was now basically shut off from completing it. The other thing was I now had to go back home.

I rebooked my return flight and headed up to the Austin airport, texting Vreeland and Lindsay along the way. I expressed hope that my job might soon be reinstated, because I sure did enjoy working with the university and Vreeland in particular. I grabbed some final tacos for the airplane, put on two masks and a face shield and lathered myself up with Purell hand sanitizer and boarded Delta flight 342 to LAX.

I took a Lyft home to see my family, scanning the Ring App for more sightings of Paul the personal trainer.

I was concerned because I have a friend, a recently divorced pal who caught his wife cheating over their shared Bluetooth account. Their cars were both on the same Bluetooth connection - which meant, when he drove into the carport, occasionally he would pick up his wife's phone conversations on his car speakers and his wife would be inside thinking she had just "lost her connection."

Unfortunately, one night when he got home, his wife's phone had clicked onto his car Bluetooth and he heard her telling their 9-year-old son's tennis instructor that she wanted him to drive his balls into her like he was returning a Roger Federer forehand.

They broke up in April.

The 'Bluetooth hijack' scenario was one I was very familiar with, having recently experienced an incredibly embarrassing moment on a family beach vacation a couple of years earlier. I had been DJ-ing a dinner party with my phone and Spotify playlist through the shared speaker that was connected to Bluetooth. At that point, after a week with my mom, stepfather, sister and about 15 nieces and nephews, I hadn't been able to find any "private time" to release sexual tension. Coupled with the fact that the entire UCLA Pi Beta Phi sorority was parading up and down the beach strand all week in barely-there thong-kinis - I had grown extremely, well... horny. One night when we were all cooking dinner, I played some of my favorite songs before realizing how truly desperate I had grown and that I needed a "release." Finding my window after serving the family asparagus, and sensing a rare opportunity of solitude, I snuck to the bathroom downstairs to watch porn and masturbate while the rest of my family sat upstairs cooking dinner.

Of course, unbeknownst, I was still hooked up to the Bluetooth speaker. So, the entire dinner party got to listen to "Blonde Bikini Babe Gets Nailed on the Beach by Old Guy" as I sat in the downstairs bathroom with my hand on my crank.

When I came upstairs, everyone was pointing and laughing at me.

Luckily my kids didn't seem to notice.

But my wife did. And I decided then and there that I was no fan of Bluetooth.

As a result, I didn't really alert my wife to the fact that I was coming home that night. I wanted to surprise her, hopefully not catching her in the act of something devious - but possibly mentally preparing myself for a moment of clarity. I had also always wanted to experience one of those "surprise your kids" viral moments when dads in the military pop out of wrapped presents and their kids go crazy. Only difference is, men in the Armed Forces are coming home after defending and fighting for our country.

I was coming home after dicking around in Austin eating bar-be-cue.

With no sight of Paul the personal trainer on the Ring, I made it home in 35 minutes and snuck through the side gate to my yard. I looked into my son's video game lair and knocked. He jumped back and smiled, opening the door and letting out a less than enthusiastic, "Hey."

Not exactly the war hero welcome I was expecting. Granted, he is 14.

My daughter's reaction was a little better, as she hugged me and said she had missed me and asked if I was back for good.

"I hope so," I said.

My wife was in the kitchen making sandwiches for the kids. I walked in and tried to give her a hug and she seemed less than surprised that I was home without warning.

"How's it going? Are you surprised I'm home?" I asked.

"Not really, I got an email alert from Delta when you boarded the flight."

"Oh." I said, forgetting that Delta always alerts family members when I fly.

There was a minute of awkward silence between us as I grabbed a sparkling water from the fridge.

"Hey... Do you think we can try and work this out? Whatever it is? Please? I feel a... distance between us and I hate it," I said.

"I don't know, Rob." She said. "Let's just see what happens the next couple of weeks... I haven't been feeling myself lately, so I'm sorry. And you heading to Austin just made me feel like I need to get out of here for a few days."

"That makes sense. It's pretty refreshing to get out of L.A."

"Well, speaking of that, I was hoping to head up north with my friend Krista this weekend. It's her 50th birthday and I need to just... get away."

I understood completely. A weekend away may just be the thing to get her juices flowing again and re-invigorate her outlook on life during this pandemic. I was pretty sure I wasn't going anywhere for awhile and I wanted to try and convince my boss at DETAIL to give me my job back. I went upstairs and took a long, hot shower.

My old boss Lawrence Freeman was willing to meet me and discuss exactly why I had been let go. After a 40 minute negotiation on where to have dinner, we met up at the French restaurant La Poubelle near my house and sat outside for happy hour. I liked the place, but the sad reality was that "La Poubelle" translated into "The Trashcan" in French.

With two burgers on the table and some happy hour beers, Lawrence told me that our parent company, CRUMB had made the ultimate decision to let me go. The arrest was terrible press for everyone involved and they even began taking down all of my old podcasts from streaming platforms.

This was bad. I had a brand that got demolished in less than 48 hours.

"Look Rob, it's just how stuff is these days," Lawrence explained. "It's Louis C. K. shit."

"But dude, I didn't sexually assault anybody!" I said.

"Yeah, but you were arrested on suspicion of murder and it got around… Having a true crime podcast expert get accused of murder is NOT exactly good for podcast ad sales - they tend to shy away from that stuff."

"Hear me out, Larry," I said. "Yesterday they arrested some other guy for this. But when I was in Austin, I started looking into this case much deeper and it goes WAY beyond a perverted panties-sniffing superintendent. I have emails from old friends, mysterious winemakers, thrift stores are somehow involved… someone broke into my hotel room and framed me, man! Trust me, there is more to this case and if you let me keep working on it, this could be DETAIL's biggest true crime podcast ever."

Lawrence sipped his beer.

"… Rob, you're amazing. We all know what you can do. But for now, I have to keep you furloughed until I can talk to CRUMB about this. And as per our deal, I will pay you one and a half month's severance and keep you on our email servers, but I can't pick up travel, hotel, expenses, none of that."

"What about what I just spent in Austin?"

"Submit that to financial, but during your severance period, we can't reimburse you for anything. No matter how many times you go back to Austin."

"Are you saying I'm allowed to go back and keep working on this case?"

"All I'm saying is that I've seen your work over the years and if you have a hunch about something, it is almost always right. But, if you go - don't expect us to foot the bill. That has to come out of pocket."

"And what if I solve this case and make the greatest podcast ever about it?"

"Then we can talk about re-hiring you."

Just then, as a glimmer of hope entered my head, I got a text message from my wife. She rarely texted me, preferring to not talk to me over the phone, so this was a surprise when it chimed onto my screen. It simply said:

Who is Alfie Adams?

CHAPTER 15

I made it home slightly buzzed, somewhat relieved to express to my wife about this mystery that was unraveling around me. I was also going to alert her that I had a chance to get my job back should I be able to solve this murder case and prove that the Austin Police Department possibly had arrested the wrong man... again.

You know what they say: Arrest the wrong man once, shame on you. Arrest another wrong man twice and shame on your entire police department.

Maybe I just made that up.

'Why was my wife asking about Alfie Adams?'

"He just called the house looking for you. I haven't answered the landline in three years, but it was a 512 area code - so I figured it was someone from Austin. He seemed nervous and weird and said that you had to call him back."

I had forgotten we even had a landline.

My wife seemed rattled.

"It sounded like someone was in trouble."

I took a deep breath and dialed Alfie's phone number back from our landline. I put him on speaker and made sure to record this conversation for the podcast. This was the type of phone call that earned you multiple seasons of shows. It rang once before he picked up.

"Hey man, long time."

My wife was correct, he did seem off. Jittery and nervous. His demeanor shifted from uncontrolled laughter to gloomy seriousness. And he was deep into many dark web conspiracy theories.

"You know why we're having so many fires around the country right now, don't you?" He asked.

"Global warming?"

"It's deeper than that, man. I'm talking gods, devils, *V for Vendetta* stuff... the end of the bad times all leading up to the heavenly creatures descending from the sky."

I had dealt with conspiracy theorists before. Some of these guys are borderline nut jobs but some them seemed to have their finger on the pulse of SOMETHING deeper. Knowledge of cover-ups, faked suicides and predicting global pandemics. I always keep an open mind when it comes to this kind of stuff, because lord knows man has still never figured out who really built the pyramids or what their purpose was in ancient times.

Also, I liked to get high and watch *Ancient Aliens*.

Anyway, Alfie went off on his tangent and then told me some information I had been waiting for. As chatty as he was becoming, I kept in mind that this guy was an accused sexual predator and had restraining orders against him from a recently murdered young girl.

"How the hell do you know Tony Valero?" Alfie whispered.

Oh man. I had forgotten that I had emailed Alfie and mentioned Tony's name. It was a catfish scheme, to get him to reveal something. Now he was coming at me with questions of his own.

"How do YOU know him?" I asked.

"What? That prick stole my girlfriend, that's how."

"And who was your girlfriend, Alfie?"

"What? Casey Dixon. I thought you knew that."

No, Alfie. And from what I remembered seeing in the UT Austin archives, she had no idea that she was your girlfriend either.

So Alfie was telling me that Casey had some sort of relationship with Tony. A relationship she had probably been in after Alfie had been slapped with a restraining order and forced to move out to Houston. But the question still lingered: Who the hell had broken into my room and sent an admission of guilt to TONY VALERO?

The questions were piling up faster than the empty beer cans I had been stacking on the kitchen counter ever since Alfie had called.

"Well, when you come back to Austin, make sure you stay away from him."

"What? Why?" I asked. "I was going to schedule a wine tasting and everything."

"Be careful," Alfie said. "That winery isn't just a winery."

I had no idea what Alfie was talking about, but it could have been one of his conspiracy theories. What else could the winery be? A time machine? A hub for alien activity? As far as I could tell, they made award winning wine and that was it.

"Hey, Alfie - When you wrote me that email, you said you had something of mine. Want to tell me what it was?" I asked.

His laugh wasn't encouraging. "Not 'til I see you next. When are you coming back to Texas?"

"I just got back to L.A."

"I'd suggest getting here as soon as possible before shit gets REALLY messy."

"Alfie, what's this all about? How did you even know I was in Austin in the first place"

"Oh, I have my ways," he said. "I'll be in touch. Also, remember:

avoid 5G towers at all costs, brother."

Alfie hung up and I sat back at my kitchen counter. This was bizarre, scary and I had to figure out why I had been dragged into this mess in the first place. Just as I thought things couldn't get any worse, my wife came in and alerted me to the latest family drama...

"Krista's 50th in wine country just got cancelled because of the fires up north," she said.

"Oh, too bad."

"Also? My mom is moving in with us for a few weeks because she's getting evacuated due to the fires in Sonoma County... and she's bringing her cat."

I was starting to wish that I had caught my wife in bed with Paul.

CHAPTER 16

I woke up early the next morning with a frantic message from Lindsay Wi. She said that after she had made us the wine tasting reservations under my name, our party was denied admittance to the Longhorn Estates property. She inquired why and they said that the name "Robert Stoner" had been on a list of banned customers.

I had never set foot in the establishment and I was already 86'd? That was a new accomplishment for me.

I called Lindsay back.

"It's weird," Lindsay said. "First they cancelled our reservation. Then, yesterday someone sent a case of Longhorn Ranch Estates wine to the journalism department apologizing for not admitting us to the tasting."

"How was the wine?"

"We gave it to some of the TA's. Vreeland didn't want us to taste it in case It was poisoned."

Oh great. Save the staff, poison the TA's.

"The other thing is, I have an in to the Austin Police Department. Are you interested in seeing any of the evidence that they have convicting the superintendent?"

"Of course I am."

"If you can get back to Austin, we can take a look at it."

I hung up and weighed my options. My wife's scheduled weekend away with Krista to celebrate her 50th in wine country was suddenly cancelled due to the Sonoma fires. And, at that moment her mom and her gigantic cat were on their way down to stay with us for an indefinite amount of time.

"Hey, Babe? I have to go back to Austin," I said, gingerly.

"You're kidding, right?"

"If I have a chance to finish this podcast up and get my job back, don't you think that's worth it?"

"You just left, Rob," she said. "What about me? Am I allowed to go anywhere? You can't just keep leaving. Both of our kids are failing math, you missed a parent-teacher conference three days ago and I haven't been able to get these kids off of electronic devices this whole time. Doing this alone sucks."

"I understand," I said, actually truly believing myself. "You have to realize that I'm onto something big here. I think this could be one of the most incredible and unique cases I've ever tackled."

She walked out of the room. This wasn't going well. I just wasn't sure how else to approach the subject. I looked over at my couch bed and noted the customized cushions that matched my mask that had started this whole freaking adventure.

"What if I go and you and the kids come with me?" I offered.

That request was met with silence. I sort of expected this to be the end. The final straw. The one-way ticket to Koreatown... Instead, she offered up a solution.

"OK. Let's do it. But I refuse to fly with Coronavirus, If we go - we take the kids and we drive."

"Really?"

"Why not? We can stay with Melissa at her house."

Melissa was an old Los Angeles friend who had moved to Austin with her kids and husband Dane 10 years earlier. She worked in the live music industry, which as you know, was devastated by Covid-19. Her income dwindled, her husband got frustrated and they couldn't seem to make it work. They legally separated a month or two ago, but since they didn't want to sell their house during the pandemic, she stayed in the main house and he moved into the guest house.

"In sickness and in health…" Guess not.

"What about your mom, though? Isn't she on her way down?"

"She can stay here while we drive out. She'll be fine. It will be nice to get out anyway. I'll tell the kids to start packing."

And just like that, I was road tripping with my family to Austin.

CHAPTER 17

It had been a year since I had driven anywhere with the family. It was up to Northern California to visit my wife's mother during the annual wine country "Grape Crush." The trip took seven and a half hours and we barely spoke the entire time. The kids sat in the back on their devices, playing games on iPads, Nintendo Switches and our iPhones once their devices died. We stopped three times, including twice at In-n-Out Burger, and listened to the Hamilton soundtrack over and over and over. And over again.

If I ever hear Pardon me, are you Aaron Burr, sir? again, I may dive head first out of a moving vehicle.

Seven and a half hours is a very doable road trip. According to my research, it was gonna take roughly 22 hours to get to Austin. That's a three-day trip stuck in a rented 2016 Subaru Forrester with my wife, who hadn't been speaking to me for the past four months and two kids who are being raised by technology and Tik Tok dancing in the back seat. This was going to be challenging.

I snuck some beer into my backpack as I loaded up the Subaru's trunk. During this pandemic, the kids had been going to school online, so leaving a Zoom class, where half of the kids tuned out and texted each other cheat codes anyway, was not a concern for either of us. They would learn more on a trip than in a virtual classroom anyway. The distance learning has been entertaining, though.

It's not everyday you hear a 5th grade teacher say, "Erin, please change your screen name from BadBitch26."

And just what would my wife and I learn from each other? Secretly, I was hoping that a trip outside of Los Angeles would be good for us. We had always traveled together and relied on it for sanity and creativity and to forget about simple issues like electric bills and broken coffee grinders. Perhaps a few days in the Lone Star State might spark something up between us. Besides, I didn't mind long road trips. I had plenty of true crime podcasts to catch up on.

We left early on Friday morning and set out down I-10 East. Luckily, we could break this trip up in Tucson, my hometown, where my mom still lived. She was overly-excited when she heard we were coming and began asking the usual questions:

"What type of food do you want?"

"How long will you be here?"

"Can you please take your God-damned baseball card collection with you when you come? I'm sick of storing it."

Sadly, I had to tell my mom that we were only stopping in for the night, as we had to continue on towards Austin. She scoffed and begged for us to stay two nights and I told her we'd play it by ear.

About two hours down the freeway, just outside of Palm Springs, I asked my wife if she wanted to listen to a true crime podcast.

"You know I hate those."

"Yeah, but it's what I do for a living... Please? Just check out the first episode. If you hate it, we'll turn it off and listen to Hamilton."

"Dear God, no," she said.

We both laughed. It was nice. Our first connection in a very long time. For the first time I felt a little something coming back to our relationship.

"Fine... One episode," she relented.

I chose to put on a podcast called *First and Nowhere* that I had done about four years earlier. The case was unique. It involved a high school football star who had been accused of murdering his cheerleader girlfriend in Taos, New Mexico. I had spent a winter there working the project and had eventually exonerated the football player and brought the real killer to justice. Turns out it was her high school chemistry teacher, a man named Tom O'Brien. Using cell phone towers and deep internet searches into the Periodic Table of the Elements, I was able to bring this case to justice. It had been a huge success and strengthened my relationship with Lawrence and DETAIL.

I fired up episode one and sat back hoping that my wife would open her mind to the podcast space. I hadn't listened to these episodes in a very long time...

Shortly before five o'clock on the afternoon of October 23, 1993, the body of Megan Jackson, a high school cheerleader from Taos, New Mexico was found in a creek near The Gorge Bar and Grill on East Plaza Road. Her arms had been bound behind her back, her body had been sexually assaulted, her throat cut -

"Jesus Christ, dad!" Came a voice from the back seat. "What the hell are you listening to?"

It was my son, chiming in about the nature of my chosen content during a family road trip. I pressed pause on the podcast app on my iPhone.

"Oops, my bad - didn't know you were listening."

We laughed. We all laughed. A lot. This was like turning a porn film on during a family movie night or something... For a second I had forgotten that what I did for a living wasn't exactly appropriate for all ages.

"I'll listen a little later," my wife said.

We drove off into the desert, past Tonopah and Red Cloud Road, where I had spent so many camping trips with friends in college, over the Colorado River and past the "Welcome to Arizona" sign that always comforted me in easier times when I could escape to Tucson to see my relatives and bathe in the monsoon season... Took the longer but prettier cut through Gila Bend, stopping to admire the pottery for sale that I had always wanted to buy but never had room for and filled the gas tank. Watched the desert paint itself red and orange and spread across the sky like so many late summer evenings of my youth... Thought about being a kid, drifting into my dreams and the day I packed it all up and moved to California. Two and a half hours later we were pulling into my mom's house and hearing the familiar crunch of gravel road beneath my car tires, reminding me of sneaking into my house late at night after hanging out with girls back in high school.

The kids ran out and said 'hi' to grandma. I started unloading the car. My wife went inside and poured herself a glass of wine.

For the first time since this pandemic hit, it felt like we were a family again.

CHAPTER 18

I hadn't heard from Vreeland since he had distanced himself from me for the sake of his department at the university. So I reached out to him via text.

Vreeland, hey man. I am coming back to Austin to finish up this podcast. The way I see it, they have the wrong man… again. By the way, see if you can snag me some of that Longhorn wine you gave to all of your TA's. I'm very intrigued.

Vreeland responded instantly:

Can't wait to see you, buddy. Lindsay showed me some stuff that she came across. I'm ready to be back in the mix here - I think what you are working on could be a game changer in podcasting. We can always put it out via the university too - we just can't pay you as much. Meaning - Nothing.

And just like that, Vreeland was back in. Thank God, I missed him.

One more thing, Stoner. I actually saved six bottles of that wine even though I told Lindsay I gave it all away. This shit is like, $50 a bottle - Do you think I'm that dumb? I'll start aerating it now.

I loved it. I went back into my childhood home to find my mom playing with her grandchildren. My wife had started setting up a game of Scrabble and my mom was already a bottle of Chardonnay in.

"Wait'll you see the two-letter words I learned from the Scrabble dictionary," my mom boasted. "It's all I've been teaching myself this whole quarantine."

We made dinner and my mom gave me my childhood collection of Mad Magazines and said to take them with me or to throw them away. I thumbed through a few of them, laughing mainly at the covers, remembering when Alfred E. Newman's face was enough to make me feel like I was on the inside track of the comedy world... I brought my son in to look at the magazines and he barely took notice. I tried to explain the genius of Don Larsen and Mort Drucker and the writing of the "usual gang of idiots" and he nodded his head twice before offering up, "Dad, the WiFi here sucks."

The Mad Magazines went into the trash.

So did the Garbage Pail Kids, the baseball cards that weren't worth anything and some few old posters and collectibles my mom had been storing for me for nearly 25 years. I threw most of it out, but I made the decision to save the Mark McGwire / Jose Canseco "Bash Brothers" poster. That shit was clean.

"Where are you putting that?" My wife inquired.

"I was thinking in the living room, like, above the dining room table?"

She laughed. It was good. Unlike the Griswold's, an all-American road trip was exactly what the Stoner family needed to feel rejuvenated.

We let the kids stay up late and my wife, my mom and I played two games of Scrabble. We lost horribly to my mom, whose flurry of two-letter words helped her score multiple points. It was impressive to hear her rattle them off.

"Mom, what the hell is a 'Za?'"

"It's slang for 'pizza.'"

"Okay, really? I'm sorry, but 'Qi' is not a word."

"Of course it is. It's the circulating life force whose properties are the basis of much of Chinese philosophy."

"Mom, you can't use 'Xu.'"

"Don't be an idiot. 'Xu' is a former minted South Vietnamese coin. That's 108 points."

Using these words alongside others, my mom destroyed us. In both games. By 150 points. My highest scoring words were "deny" on a triple-word score and "kill" on a triple letter. I lost by 158.

We stayed up late. It was nice. The moon was shining down as we murdered more wine and my mom even put the kids to bed for us. As my wife and I sat outside staring up at the stars for the first time in a long while, I felt like telling her how this entire ordeal began. I wanted to come clean. I wanted to mention that I had been tempted by this young girl and followed her to her apartment and how she was ready to do very bad things with me. About how I shunned her advances and left... And how she was killed 45 minutes later. I hadn't been sleeping much since this incident and I felt like the truth might set me free. I thought that if I opened up, maybe she would tell me exactly what was happening with Paul the personal trainer. I took a moment to gather my thoughts and just as I was about to open up the conversation, my mom burst into the back yard.

"Kids are asleep. Who wants to watch our idiot president on the news?"

CHAPTER 19

We woke up in my childhood bedroom the next morning around 11. Somehow, I had drunkenly hung up the "Bash Brothers" poster on the wall. I did it as a way to guarantee that I'd be back around someday - and also I did it to torture my mom a little.

It's just how we do around my poor mom's house. My sister has had the same New Kids on the Block poster in her room since 1989.

I drank some coffee and read an actual newspaper for the first time in about a decade and started getting things ready. My mom started asking if the kids could stay while we went on to Austin.

"Come on, Rob. I haven't seen them in seven months."

After a long discussion with the kids, who all agreed that some time getting spoiled at grandma's would be more fun than watching daddy track down a murder suspect in Texas, we agreed to let them stay in Tucson. We settled on four days, which might be enough to solve this case, but in reality, probably would not. My wife said if I was still languishing in the podcast, she would happily drive back early and scoop them up.

Grandma needed it, we needed the time away and Austin wasn't exactly much of a kid's town. We made some sandwiches, packed it all up and kissed the kids good-bye. Just before we were about to drive off, my son ran up to the car window and begged us to reconsider leaving him…

"Dad, I'm serious, the WiFi here REALLY sucks."

13 hours to Austin. It was currently 1:30 so if we powered through, we could make it by 4 or 5 AM the next morning. I was pretty sure we would be getting a cheap motel somewhere along the way. I was not one for long drives and no matter how many podcasts I put on, eventually I would fall asleep at the wheel.

About an hour into the drive, my Ring camera alert went off. Motion at your front. Who could that be? Paul the trainer unaware that we had split town? An intruder? When I looked at my phone, it became clear as to who had just arrived at our house seeking room and board. My mother-in-law and her 250 pound cat.

No, her cat is not an exotic jungle cat. It's a house cat… but HOUSE is the operative word here, as it must literally weigh close to 125 pounds. It smells like shit, meows loudly and has a Christmas bell tied around its neck to guarantee that you start dreading the upcoming holidays every time you hear this ratted beast lumber through the hallway. She claims the bell helps birds and mice escape the cat when it closes in for an attack, which basically goes against the cat's natural instincts so instead, it chews on computer cords and kid toys and occasionally trashes its own litter box. Whenever my mother-in-law has visited in the past, I have prayed to God to transport me anywhere else.

We drove through the middle of the 110-degree desert looking at billboards promoting bizarre roadside attractions like "The Thing," which is essentially a mummified mother and child from the 1800's stuffed in the back of a Shell Station convenience store. For decades, literature and television has recognized "The Thing" for its strange appeal that has brought in motorists and tourists since the 1960's. "The Thing" museum also boasts a display of a Rolls Royce that was apparently once owned by Adolf Hitler, so I try to avoid fueling up there whenever I'm in the area.

My wife called her mom and gave her directions about the door locks, the new coffee maker and everything else we had upgraded during the pandemic. We warned her against using flushable wipes, letting the cat upstairs and which light switches needed to be flipped on for certain outlets to work. She thanked us for letting her visit and my wife asked how long she would be staying with us.

"I don't know, a month or so? At least until the fires die down."

Looks like I'd be in Austin a lot longer than four days.

CHAPTER 20

The monkey on my back was still riding me hard. Should I tell my wife about following Casey Dixon to her apartment? Part of me thought that a long road trip was exactly the place to reveal this type of secret, but another part imagined my wife kicking me out of the car and stranding me on a highway outside of El Paso.

The drive was fairly easy, and the lack of traffic was a welcome relief. I finally got my wife to listen to a true crime podcast I had produced and she proceeded to share two straight hours of Howard Stern with me.

Eventually, we settled on a Jason Isbell Spotify playlist.

I decided that as we crossed Texas state lines, I would tell her the whole story. Long road trips have a way of doing this to people. You share your innermost secrets. Back in college, I once drove to Oregon with my freshman roommate and he admitted that he liked to masturbate while watching me sleep.

I moved out two days later.

The story I was about to tell my wife was not going to be an easy one, but I figured that I still had the one ace up my sleeve. The Ring camera. Paul the personal trainer. His six-and-a-half hour visit during my stay in Austin was still weighing heavy on my mind. If I came clean about Casey, maybe my wife would come clean about Paul.

"So I have to tell you something," I started. "I wasn't exactly honest about what happened in Austin."

Oh the anxiety. The pressure. The nerves. I hated all of this. My stomach dropped.

"What are you talking about?" My wife countered.

"Remember how I told you I was a witness in that murder at my hotel?"

"Yeah."

"Well, as it turns out, I was sort of set up. By someone... to look like I had been the killer."

"What the fuck are you talking about?"

Oh boy. Telling my wife that you were a murder suspect in the middle of a deserted highway may not have been the smartest idea. And now I was going to lower the boom even further.

"I was partying with this girl and... I basically went to her apartment. She sort of wanted to fool around - but NOTHING happened, I swear - it was just like, flattering you know?"

Silence. The dry heat of the Texas road blew through the cracked window beneath the hushed tones of Jason Isbell's Dreamsicle.

"Why did you go to her apartment?"

"I don't know. I guess I didn't want to go to bed and I had been cooped up in our house for so long with this pandemic and I just wanted to feel something different. BUT I left the minute I got up there... Like, immediately... And I don't know - things have been so weird between us, I've been sleeping on the couch - I don't know but I'm so sorry - "

"Why are you even telling me this?"

"Well..." I thought long and hard before sharing this doozy of a response. "She was murdered 45 minutes after I left her apartment."

The next 25 minutes were pretty silent as I waited for some sort of response from my wife. I counted billboards, darted my eyes across the landscape and entered a strange dream-like state. The dream was not a good one.

I wasn't sure how, but I looked down and saw that whereas I was formerly driving around 80 I was now suddenly driving 65 miles per hour. I had somehow lost 15 miles per hour on my RPM and possibly 15 years of my marriage.

"I have to tell you something too," my wife said, finally breaking the awkward stillness.

I knew what was coming. Paul the trainer...

"Do you remember my trainer, his name is Paul - "

"I KNEW it, you slept with him!"

"What?" She screamed.

I was livid. I pulled my car over to the side of the road and nearly lost my mind.

"I SAW the Ring footage - He was there for SIX HOURS! Six hours! We don't even have a workout room, AND the kids said he stayed for dinner - "

She had left the car and was pacing into the desert.

"What are you doing?" I yelled.

"You spoke to the KIDS about this?"

"What happened?"

"You're an IDIOT, you know that?" She screamed.

I did know that. And it wasn't the last time I would hear it.

"Yeah - Paul's a personal trainer," she said with an edge of hatred. "He's also a handyman. So, that day he came over and fixed that beam in the back, planted my flowers, fixed the broken gate, re-set the sprinklers and fixed a fucking clogged toilet. ALL the shit YOU said you were going to do but you just never did. I paid him $250 bucks and he left. Happy?"

Oh shit. Yeah, our house had a lot of problems. I never got around to fixing any of them.

"So what was it you wanted to tell me?" I asked.

She stopped pacing and took a deep breath. I felt around in my pocket and pulled out that pack of American Spirit cigarettes. There were nine left. I lit one up as she grimaced in my direction.

"I don't even want to know when you started smoking again," she said.

"The night that girl was killed."

"Oh Jesus Christ."

"What did you want to tell me?"

Another moment. A small plane passed by overhead. The clouds were blooming into majestic southwestern patterns. They were Mark Maggiori clouds, my favorite painter.

"Look. After Paul stayed for dinner he sort of... Well - on the way out he - sort of tried to kiss me."

I looked at the ground. Some sort of lizard scurried near my flip flops.

"And what did you do?" I murmured.

"What do you mean? I told him that I was married and he apologized and he went home."

"That's it?"

"Yes, that's it." She said. "Is that what happened with the girl in her apartment?"

"Yes. I swear on our children's lives - yes."

"Then I swear on our children's lives as well."

In a screenplay they would call this moment a "BEAT." The actors gather their breaths, their thoughts and their voices. They look around at the blue skies surrounding them and take a deep breath of Covid-friendly air... And then. ..

She smiled at me with that smile. The one I remembered from our wedding day. The look of hope from our innocent youth. That smile that she had flashed when she met our children for the first time. She was the most beautiful creature I had ever seen. I saw a glimmer in her face that possibly meant that she was seeing the same thing in me, but I wasn't sure. All I knew was that this had been a long time coming. We were getting to know each other again. No more secrets, no more lies... Maybe I could even go back into the bed again. I knew I needed to say something to break the silence. Instead she did.

"Can we please go to a hotel somewhere and have makeup sex?"

I took out my phone and started looking for the nearest town.

Van Horn, Texas boasts of having a two-star Red Range Inn and is best known for being the place where Jeff Bezos bought 300 acres of land to launch his space tourism project about a decade ago. The town had a population of just under 2,500 people - which was half the size of my high school - and according to the website Yelp, the second best restaurant option in town was a Subway.

We drove in around 7:30, bought wine and beer from a mini mart and checked into the Red Range Inn. $66.00. A far cry from the Hotel San Joaquin.

We began tearing our clothes off. I couldn't remember how long it had been, but it felt good. It was like old times. We pressed our bodies against each other, giggling like high school kids trying this for the first time, barely speaking and pretty much ignoring any foreplay. We worked it out on the bed, climaxing and rolling off each other laughing and reminding ourselves how we used to be so great together. This was good.

Although there was a pretty good chance that she was thinking of Paul.

Lying there in the ruins of our pleasure, I realized that I wasn't thinking about Austin at all. For the first time in two weeks my mind was completely clear. Life was as good as it could be during this pandemic.

And then, I received a text alert from Vreeland over at the University. I picked up my phone and read his message:

Hey - Bad news. Alfie Adams is dead.

CHAPTER 21

I didn't sleep much that night, although the cheap mini mart wine helped knock me out for a few hours. I awoke to find my wife showered and ready to go, as if our act of passion the night before had re-energized her. I felt energized too, but I don't think it was because of our sexual experience. All I was thinking about was Alfie Adams.

With roughly seven hours to Austin, I had time to start figuring this mystery out. First call was to Vreeland. I had my wife record our conversation on her phone. This was the type of shit that makes true crime podcasts work.

"What happened, Vreeland?" I asked.

"As far as I know, it was an overdose. Fentanyl or something."

"I'm not surprised, that guy was in outer space when I spoke to him."

"The crazy thing is, he wrote a letter to the Austin Chronicle saying that he was fearing for his life. A friend of mine in the editorial department got me a copy of the letter, want me to read it?"

"Does a one-legged duck swim in a circle?"

Vreeland laughed. Glad he still had his sense of humor. He got into Alfie's letter to the Chronicle.

To whom it may concern,

My name is Alfred Felix Adams and I am in fear for my life. I am concerned that somebody may be coming after me. Last week my ex-girlfriend, Casey Dixon was found dead in her apartment. She had been strangled and I believe you may have the wrong suspect in custody. There are others you must look into. Thrift store owners. Winemakers. Journalists. Until then, as the fires rage across our country, I await the arrival of sky creatures to cleanse the Earth.

Best,

Alfred Adams. September 6, 2020

"Guy was a total nut job," I said. "Sky creatures?"

"Right?" Vreeland responded. "Thing is, he predicted he would turn up dead. Why would he mention winemakers having anything to do with it?"

"Not sure. All I know is I wouldn't drink that wine that Tony Valero sent over."

"Well, none of my colleagues are dead yet, so I'm assuming it's fine."

"You're a heck of a role model," I said. "Do us a favor? Have Lindsay book us a tasting at Longhorn Creek Vineyard as soon as she can and do it under your name, not mine. For some reason I'm not allowed into any vineyards where I've never been let into in the first place."

"Sounds good. Call me when you get here."

I hung up and told my wife to stop recording the conversation.

"What was that all about?" She asked.

"It's a long story, but an old friend is dead, he mentioned the name of a suspect that I was already suspicious of and it looks like we're going wine tasting when we get to Austin."

"Texas has a wine country?"

"I know, right?"

For the rest of the drive, I laid out the case for her. She had as many questions as I did. Who had been in my room sending emails the night Casey was killed? Why did Casey lure me to her apartment? Who had killed her? Was Alfie's death foul play? How was Tony Valero involved? In my dream world, she would join the hunt with me and help me bring this podcast to a conclusion. In reality, I knew she would be spending most of her Austin time with Melissa.

I flashed back to that European tour in 2003. Alfie's band had opened for us one night in Barcelona and after numerous bottles of Sangria, Alfie had spilled an ashtray in a nightclub where he had politely been over-served. Two angry Spaniards came after him and threatened to beat him up. When they caught him, it took some heavy negotiating to get him out of their clutches. Having been raised in a border town I spoke the most Espanol out of all of us - and when I finally was able to translate what they were saying, I had offered 100 Euros for his freedom.

"Tu amigo es hombre muerto," Spanish Badass Number One said.

My Spanish wasn't as polished as it had been in high school, but I knew "hombre muerto" roughly translated to "Dead man."

"Por favor, no mata este hombre. Aquí es 100 Euro… " I said in broken Sonoran desert Spanish. I was basically telling them not to kill Alfred and that I had 100 Euros for their trouble.

"Nos quedaremos con tu reloj," one of them yelled.

Reloj? Shit. That meant watch. I happened to have been traveling with a Navajo turquoise sterling silver watch band that framed a pretty cheap timepiece. It wasn't about the value, it was about the fact that the watch had been my grandfather's, who had worked part time in an antique store in Sedona, Arizona. When he had passed away in 2000, he didn't have much left, but the piece I was always drawn to was his watch. It had been valued at about $300 by a dealer, but it wasn't exactly the price I was concerned about. It was the sentimentality of the whole thing. At that point I regretted even bringing it to Europe with me, but it was a definite conversation piece and looked great on stage.

"Come on, man… this was my grandfather's," I said in plain English.

"Tu Reloj."

I looked at Alfie and hated him for getting us in this position. What kind of douchebag turns over an ashtray in a bar in a foreign country? I shook my head as they tightened their forearm choke against his neck. I slowly removed my watch and handed it over. They took the $100 Euros too, ran off and Alfie dropped to the floor gasping for his breath. As they ran away they yelled, "Ni se te ocurra volver a nuestro bar, maricona"

I wasn't sure what that meant, but I knew 'maricona' wasn't a very kind word. In any language.

I wondered if the "thing" Alfie was going to return to me was somehow my grandpa's watch band. I doubted it. Unless he had somehow tracked down those two Spanish assholes and retrieved it all those years ago. Now that Alfie was dead, I guess I'd never find out.

Alfie re-paid me the 100 Euros immediately, after his parent's put more money in his bank account. He often picked up bar tabs and band meals even though he was playing the "broke starving musician" role. In reality, his dad was a pediatrician and his mother a school teacher. That was back when Alfie was somewhat normal… before the "sky creatures," the opiates and the 5G Tower conspiracy theories.

The miles rolled away and my wife and I drifted in and out of conversation. She seemed happy and was looking forward to getting together with Melissa in Austin and we both continually mentioned that we really missed the children. After calling them over FaceTime and hearing that they were having a really great time with grandma, we inched closer to Austin and I phoned the La Quince Inn and made a reservation for that night.

Nearly 15 minutes after the reservation was made, Lawrence called me.

"Rob, I hear you're heading back to Austin."

"Yessir. I'm gonna finish this podcast and get my damn job back."

"Yeah, about that... Look - We have a project in the works with the musician, humorist and mystery writer Kinky Friedman. You know him?"

"Of course I know who Kinky Friedman is. What's the project?"

"We're turning a few of his mystery novels into podcasts. We need someone to go make contact and interview him, get some stuff for an EPK. He has a ranch down in Medina where he lives with like, ten dogs and an armadillo or something."

"Are you saying I have a job again?"

"Let's just do this one on a freelance agreement, does that work? I don't think CRUMB is ready to hire you back yet."

"Of course I'll do it! I'm about an hour outside of Austin right now. When's the interview?"

"He can do Wednesday if you can. I'm emailing you his manager's information."

"Hey Lawrence, thanks dude. This is awesome. One question, though... Can I expense this trip?"

There was a long pause on the other side of the line. I looked at my wife and prayed that he would agree. After all, with no income, I suddenly found myself much more aware of my financial instability.

"Sure," he said. "But don't go overboard."

And just like that I cancelled my room at the La Quince Inn and made a new reservation at the Hotel San Joaquin.

CHAPTER 22

Not much had changed since I left town. The Hotel San Joaquin outdoor lounge was filling up with the hipster elite. The pool had its regulars. In a beautiful yet disturbing tribute, a memorial photograph of Casey Dixon had been placed in the lobby. My wife and I arrived under the radar and I said hello to Mike Porter - the friendly manager in the expensive and uncomfortable hipster clothes. He had added a new turquoise ring and a flowing Indian-inspired scarf. He was overly anxious to welcome me back to the hotel and gave me a couple of free drink tickets before asking me how my podcast on Casey's murder was going. I mentioned that one of my original suspects was now dead. He shook his head, said "Crazy world" and handed me that stupid 70's-era hotel keychain for room 30.

"We haven't rented out room 25 since Casey was killed," he said. "Police say it's still a location of interest to them. Any leads?"

"A few… but nothing concrete," I said.

"Well, yeah - I'm sure it's something easier than you think. I heard she had a stalker."

"You may be right, Mike," I said. "I'm going to get to the bottom of this. Trust me."

"Appreciate you, man. Have a nice stay."

My wife made her way through the lobby and passed by the photo of Casey. She stopped.

"Pretty girl," she said. "I don't know how you turned that down..."

We walked past the lounge and pool and unlocked room 30. I wasn't sure if we were going to have a repeat performance from last night, but it didn't matter. My mind was racing. I wanted to get in touch with Vreeland and I texted him asking him to meet me at the San Joaquin lounge.

We going big tonight?

He texted back. *Can't. My wife's with me.*

Vreeland showed up to the bar with two bottles of the Longhorn Creek Estates wine that the vineyard had sent to the journalism department. I looked them over, thinking that their graphic design and labels seemed somewhat damaged and uneven - as if they had been steamed off of another bottle and applied to this batch. I immediately became suspicious that this wine may have actually been tampered with and pointed out the label inconsistencies to Vreeland. He looked it over and said that he wasn't able to tell.

A second later, Lindsay walked through the door. Lindsay! I had forgotten about how helpful she had been earlier. And according to Vreeland, she had been doing some new research. She joined us in the fateful Hotel San Joaquin lounge for a drink until I quickly realized I was in no shape to function there.

"I'm sorry guys, can we go somewhere else? This place still gives me the creeps," I said.

Everybody agreed and we headed up to Stereo for socially distanced beers in the outdoor patio. My wife and Lindsay seemed to get along and after about 15 minutes of discussing the case, my wife called herself a Lyft.

"This has been fun and all, but I'm going to go visit my friend Melissa," she said.

She kissed me good-bye, put her mask back on and jumped in an Uber.

Vreeland ordered us two more beers.

"You guys mind if I record this conversation?" I asked.

"Of course not," Vreeland said. "That's what we do."

I put my iphone on the table and opened the Recorder app.

I hit the record button and listened as Lindsay broke down the death of Alfie Adams.

"Alfie's cause of death was acute intoxication of opioids. He had fentanyl, Xanax and traces of marijuana in his system," she said. "And, the police tracked down his family. They're on their way here tomorrow to go through his apartment."

"Is there any way we can go through it with them?" I asked. "Maybe look for some clues?"

"I guess we could stop by and say he was our friend and that we had left stuff there or something. I'm just not sure that his parents want to meet with anybody."

"Well the good news is, in 2003 I toured with the guy for six weeks - like, a lifetime ago," I offered. "I actually WAS his friend."

"That helps," said Vreeland.

"And what about Valero?" I continued.

"We booked a wine tasting for Wednesday evening," Vreeland said.

"Shit. I'm driving down to Kinky Friedman's ranch Wednesday... I doubt I'll be back by then."

"Oh yeah, that's going to be awesome."

As it turned out, Vreeland was the original creative behind the Kinky Friedman podcast, along with an old friend of mine from L. A. named Mark Dawson. I faintly recalled him pitching it to me a week-and-a-half earlier, but he reminded me that this was actually his original idea. He had pitched the audio book platform to Lawrence at

DETAIL during the 10 days I was gainfully unemployed.

DETAIL gave it the green light.

"Kinky's stories are going to make great podcasts... we've secured the rights to five of them," he said.

I nodded, took out my pack of American Spirits and said I was excited about the opportunity.

"Still smoking those, huh?" Vreeland said.

"I know. I hate it."

"Hey, with Kinky - you never know. He solved a lot of crimes in his books back in the day, maybe he can help us out with this one."

I laughed. Kinky was probably swimming in a gold plated pool watching the world burn around him.

"Yeah, we'll see," I said.

Lindsay then produced a manila envelope that she had been holding back from sharing with me. She wasn't sure if I could stomach the images inside, so she had waited until I was a little oiled up on good old Texas IPA before producing the materials.

"So, this is the other thing I wanted to show you," she said. "These are files and crime photos from the night Casey Dixon was killed."

I gingerly took them from her hand and shook out the materials. Immediately, I could see why she was holding them back.

The first thing that caught my eye was the Austin Chronicle headline. It was less than sensational, but provided some clarity into the bumbling actions of the Austin Police Department.

Suspect Arrested in South Austin Murder Was Building Superintendent; First Suspect Released.

Luckily, they did not use my name.

The name of the superintendent murder suspect was Roberto Arenas, a 44-year-old second generation Texan whose dad had served in the fire department. The crime photos of the scene somewhat resembled the terrific Los Angeles noir photo book "LAPD '53" by James Ellroy. Through Ellroy's hard-boiled writing, you get slowly introduced to the intense crime wave that passed over the City of Angels in that one particularly violent year. Each write-up is accompanied by thorough black and white police photographs of weapons, shot-up liquor stores and dead bodies.

The first photo I saw was in black and white. I immediately recognized a fairly clear snapshot of Casey's bedroom - featuring a faint outline of her poor lifeless body lying on the ground with the floor-length Target mirror toppled over to her left.

From the right hand corner of the wall I could scarcely make out a lock of Harry Styles' hair.

As I examined the photos and notes, looking in closely hoping to find any other clues, I noticed one thing that seemed somewhat familiar stashed in the corner of the kitchen where the struggle undoubtedly took place... I made out an empty cardboard box with a familiar wine label logo on it.

Longhorn Creek Estates.

I suddenly flashed back to the night I had followed Casey upstairs. She had poured me a glass of old wine... was it from a bottle of Longhorn Creek? I was so fragile and nervous at the time, I hadn't paid attention.

Reading deeper into the story, the police had mentioned that they had searched the superintendent's apartment and uncovered a pair of women's undergarments belonging to Ms. Dixon. They had also found a piece of rope matching the exact same type that was found around Casey's neck. Oddly enough, the murder weapon was polypropylene rope, the "yellow cord" used by boaters to tow water skiers, wakeboarder and dinghies in the water.

Why the hell would Roberto Arenas have polypropylene sitting around? Did he own a watercraft I wasn't aware of? Austin was full of recreational lakes, so if he did have a fun speedboat or something parked up by Lake Austin or Lake Travis, it could make sense... but otherwise, that type of rope was rarely seen outside of water-adjacent areas.

The final confusing piece was when they listed certain cryptic text messages she had sent earlier that night taken from her phone.

This information was not yet released to the public.

This should be easy, he was already flirting with me at the bar earlier.

And...

Please don't tell anyone at work what is going on.

The number on the receiving end of those texts? Mike Porter: the manager of the Hotel San Joaquin. Suddenly, that friendly guy in his $500 flat-brimmed cowboy hat and new turquoise ring didn't seem so friendly anymore...

CHAPTER 23

Alfie Adams' apartment was pretty disgusting.

I am not apartment shaming or whatever 'Cancel Culture' would call my description in these strange times, especially since Alfie was a recently deceased young man. But this place was putrid. Like most artists, I have lived in some pretty feculent joints in my life as well, including a Hoover Street apartment in South Central Los Angeles in the 90's that had a family of possums living in the oven, but this place was off-the-wall filthy. I had no idea that Alfie had been this down-and-out.

Alfie's place was in a UT apartment called the "Sienna" barely 1000 yards off of campus. His plants were dead, his fridge was a rusted shit box from 1982 and his front door had a Sublime sticker on the front of it that had probably been there since 1995.

The Adams family had arrived around 10 AM. It was about 11:15 and a good amount of Alfie's stuff had been overturned and certain keepsakes taken outside. A few art books, some framed photos and a bicycle.

Vreeland, Lindsay and I met Alfie's parents in the grassy area as they were leaving the apartment building. Dr. Richard and Bonnie Adams were fairly respectable folks from Chicago, but their grief was real and hard to fathom. Alfie was their oldest child and even though he hadn't quite found his way in life, he was their wayward son and they were very happy to meet us.

"We weren't sure if he had many friends," Bonnie said. "It's nice to meet you three."

I felt pretty awful about calling myself a "friend," but luckily I relayed some stories about our trip to Europe in 2003, our recent phone conversation and how I had possibly left some stuff in the apartment last time I had "visited." Bonnie hugged me. She then proceeded to show me some of the other stuff they had gathered from his place.

A few drawings, a belt with a skull buckle. An older bass guitar that was missing a string.

As we went through a few boxes, Bonnie said something disturbing.

"It's just so sad that his fiancee died last week, too… such a tragedy."

"I'm sorry, his fiancee?" I inquired.

"Her name was Casey Dixon… she was murdered."

I was tempted to play an eerie note on the three-stringed bass guitar.

Vreeland and Lindsay went through some of the stuff in Alfie's apartment, looking through drawers and his closet. Eventually, they came across a shoebox that had been hidden up in the right nook. When we opened it up, a lot of things suddenly became clear.

Inside were hundreds of photos of Casey Dixon. Photographs from high school and college, all printed from her Instagram account. Long-lensed photos, as if he had been stalking and spying on her. What was at the bottom, however, was the most disturbing. A pair of women's underwear, which may or may not have been Casey's.

"This was one sick puppy," Vreeland said.

"Well, either he had fabricated this relationship with Casey in his mind, or they were actually engaged and Casey just wasn't aware of it. Either way, the dude had a thing for her," Lindsay remarked.

Ya think?

In the medicine cabinet I found some pills, but nothing indicating that he had been abusing any prescription drugs as well as a toothbrush that looked as if it was last used to recently scrub World War II submarines. The toilet was missing a knob on the seat and the shower had a permanent ring against its white basin.

Finally, Lindsay turned up something from under the bed.

"Rob, I think you should see this."

I moved over to his fairly elevated Futon and Lindsay handed me a manila envelope. On the top was my name, written in black marker.

ROB STONER. Los Angeles, CA.

I slid my finger underneath the enclosure and lifted the top flap.

There was a note inside:

Rob, I never got to thank you properly back in Spain. I tracked you down a few years ago after listening to your true crime podcasts - I think you're a great host and writer/producer and I think I can help you solve cases in the future. I have a vast understanding of how criminal minds work. Please call me when you're in Austin. I'm also enclosing something I believe you've been missing for a long time.

Best, Alfie

I dug my hand deeper into the envelope and pulled out what he was talking about.

Holy shit. It was my grandfather's watch.

CHAPTER 24

"I'm just amazed that he tracked it down," I told my wife back at the Hotel San Joaquin. "It's weird. 17 years ago this thing disappeared into the Spanish evening and I thought I'd never see it again."

"Well, based on that box of photos he had of your girlfriend Casey he had done some fairly aggressive spy work in the past."

"I guess. The question is, how did he find those guys? And how delusional was Alfie to tell his parents he was engaged?"

"Crazy people have a way of doing that," she said. "I had a stalker in college."

"Didn't we all."

We called the kids and then went to get some coffee from Momo's next door. I finally took some time away from my thoughts on this entire situation and asked my wife how it was hanging out with Melissa the day before.

"I want to move here," she announced.

Excuse me?

"Think about it, Rob. L.A. is a mess, the schools suck, and I haven't seen stars in the sky like this pretty much ever. We could sell our place and buy something by Melissa's and send our kids to high school here and you can work remotely, right?"

I sipped my coffee and stared out on Congress Street, focusing on the obnoxious vintage truck that the hotel had refurbished and painted with their logo on it.

"Can we talk about it after I solve this case?"

"Well, if it's okay with you, I'm going to check out some places for sale today."

This discussion was one we've had before. It happens every time we travel outside of Los Angeles... We start looking for places and contemplate the big move out of the City of Angels. In the past ten years, we have looked at houses in Nashville, Seattle, Tucson, New York, Aspen, Lake Oswego, Greece, Sonoma County and during one peculiar road trip, Daphne, Alabama. (We passed on that one after I spotted a Nazi flag in our future neighbor's backyard).

Out of all these places, Austin had the most appeal, but I wasn't in the mindset to start house hunting just yet. I told Melissa to let my wife have fun looking but reminded her that I still didn't have my job back.

As she grabbed a Lyft and scurried off to find our next home in the Austin suburbs, I decided to head over to Vreeland's campus and watch him teach a Zoom class from an empty office.

The class had shrunk since the last time I had sat in, with about 15 less students than before.

"What happened to all your students?" I asked Vreeland.

"Frat party last week. 100 kids got Coronavirus at some Lambda Pi rager. Frat got suspended, half of my classes were cut in half."

Holy shit. I thought about how tough it would be to go to college during this pandemic. I wondered if I would have been the type to risk my health by attending some big fraternity party. Thinking back to a night when I shared a bottle of wine with a homeless guy following a Neil Young concert in Santa Barbara, I figured that, yeah. .. I would have.

Vreeland asked me if I wanted to talk to the students for a second, as one of them was having trouble with her own project, a podcast idea about people who have had relatives who have been murdered or killed. I gave her some advice.

"Are there similarities between people you've interviewed who have relatives who have met tragic ends?" I proposed.

"Well, a lot of them want to know the full story and get closure. Like the guy who wrote that book about The Potato Masher Murder based on his great-grandmother's killing."

"Closure, huh?" I said, beginning to think that there was going to be no closure to this Casey Dixon case at all.

"There's always more than one suspect in the unsolved cases," she said.

Hmm. More than one suspect. At this point, my main suspect was Alfie - who was dead. The superintendent was currently carving his initials into the wall of a cell at Travis State Prison and I still had no idea how Tony Valero or Mike Porter played into this whole scenario.

Vreeland and I finished up his class, masked up and walked over to the cafe to meet Lindsay. On the way I received an email from Robert Mandelbaum, the lawyer who helped me out on that day I was arrested.

It was a bill for $5,000.

CHAPTER 25

Vreeland and I discussed possible scenarios as Lindsay typed into her laptop. She was communicating with Detective Hernandez, the detective at the Austin Police department who had been the one to cuff me back on my arrest day. He had written her back from an earlier inquiry.

As far as we are concerned, this case is closed. Thank you for checking in with me.

This type of stuff always happened in the true crime podcasts I had done in the past. The police give up and the wrong man rots in jail. Then people like me start buzzing around trying to solve the real murder.

"Maybe it simply WAS the superintendent," Vreeland said.

"Roberto Arenas? I just don't think it's that easy."

"What if Alfie killed her and then killed himself because he couldn't live with it?" Vreeland proposed.

"That makes sense, but why would he have tracked ME down?

It wasn't just for that watch. .. And who sent Tony Valero that email from my laptop?"

"Who had a key to your room?"

"What if it was Mike Porter, the hotel manager?" I said. "Remember, Casey did text him late that night."

The waitress dropped a quesadilla on our table and refilled our water glasses.

"We gotta go talk to Mike Porter," Vreeland said.

The Hotel San Joaquin was fairly empty when we arrived back around 3: 30. Tuesdays in Austin during a pandemic weren't particularly good party nights, although a bunch of women with shopping bags did walk through as if they were checking in for a long bachelorette weekend.

"This town will be like Nashville soon if we're not careful," Vreeland said. "First come these idiots, then the pedal bikes with a bunch of drunk girls drinking and blasting Luke Bryan songs. It's only a matter of time."

We sent Lindsay to the front desk to talk to Mike Porter. Unfortunately, he wasn't there. Vreeland stepped away for an office hours visit over Zoom on his phone with a student, so I went to my hotel room and recorded a few notes into my computer before deciding to make a little phone call to the hotel. I hit record on my device and went back into my Detective Sproles voice and as I dialed the front desk.

"Hotel San Joaquin, this is Rachel."

"Hi ma'am, this is Detective Nick Sproles from the Austin Police Department. Do you have a minute?"

"Um, sure?"

"Your manager, Mike Porter -- are you aware that he is a suspect in the murder of your co-worker Casey Dixon?"

"Mike is what? No!"

"Is Mr. Porter there now?"

"Tuesday is his day off, he hangs out at Lake Travis, I'm pretty sure that's where he's posting on his IG from."

"His Instagram? Can you share his handle?"

"Yeah, it's @porterdisorder. He usually blows up his stories on lake days."

I thanked Rachel for her time and went back out to sit with Lindsay. I had Lindsay follow @porterdisorder so it didn't look weird that I had randomly followed him and we opened up his account. As it turned out, @porterdisorder wasn't shy about his #LakeLife. To mis-quote the late great Warren Zevon, Porter Disorder was in the house. Mike Porter was definitely at the lake that afternoon, and he was knee-boarding, jumping off of the rails, drinking beers and partying, mask-less I might add, with about five girls who were "Boomeranging" themselves in thongs on his Instagram feed. There were a number of action shots and bikini pictures to observe, but as we examined them closely, I wasn't focusing on the fact that a taut, young pretty Texas girl was posing in a bathing suit on the back of a boat. Something else had caught my eye...

The polypropylene rope pulling the knee-board looked an awful lot like the weapon that had been used to strangle Casey Dixon.

CHAPTER 26

A second bill from Mandelbaum showed up in my inbox that night. Five. Thousand. Dollars. The guy had been in my presence for roughly five hours, as far as I could tell, so he was charging me a grand-an-hour. Not bad work if you can get it, I guess. Still, I had no way of paying this bill and decided to phone Mandelbaum myself. He answered drunk, which only solidified that he was my type of lawyer. I pressed record on my computer because in podcast research you really never know what you're going to hear.

"Hey Mandelbaum, it's Rob Stoner... the guy you helped get off from the Casey Dixon murder?

"Ah, yeah yeah - how are ya man?"

"Well, to tell you the truth, I'm not great. I'm looking at a five thousand dollar bill from you here."

"You're welcome."

"Huh?" Clearly, I was confused.

"I only charged you for my retainer. I gave you the friends and family discount on that one."

"That's a DISCOUNT?" I shouted.

"Well, look at the alternatives. You could have been rotting away at Travis State right now cuddling with your new cellmate."

"Good point."

"We can work out a payment plan, don't worry about it," he said. "Crazy that I'm still involved in this case, isn't it?"

"You're still involved? What are you talking about?"

"I've been consulting with the superintendent they are holding in the murder. Guy's name is Roberto Arenas. He doesn't know WHAT is going on, but all clues seem to be working against us. Murder weapon, the poor girl's underwear... it's pretty bad."

"Hey - quick question. Where did your client go the day of the murder?"

"I'm not at liberty to discuss my client's personal -"

"C'mon Mandelbaum this could help your case. I'm having a hard time believing that Roberto was involved. I have another suspect in mind that might clear his name."

Mandelbaum took a deep breath. I heard the sound of him drinking something on the other line. To my trained ear it sounded like a scotch and soda.

"Well, he works part-time as a handyman on some other properties when he's not managing the apartment building, so he claims he spent most of the day of the murder out in Hill Country."

"What's in the Hill Country?" I asked.

"Some winery he occasionally works at... It's called Longhorn Creek."

Shit.

"What about a boat? Does he own a boat by any chance?"

"Probably not, he had to sell his 1997 Toyota Tercel just to hire me."

"Thanks man," I said."I'll have your money someday."

I hung up before he could respond.

I got in my car and drove to the nearest mini mart, a place called Dom's Market on Riverside. The place was like a hipster grocery store, and surprise surprise - they sold their own merch. T-shirts, bandannas, wine glasses and corkscrews... They also happened to sell Longhorn Creek wine. I bought a bottle of their Texas Cabernet for $39. 99 and after examining the label, decided that the bottles sent to Vreeland were definitely NOT from this same winery. Great. Forged wine labels. Another mystery. I got home to the hotel just as my wife came in, a little wine-buzzed and excited about her afternoon house-hunting.

"I found us a place! It's sooo charming and totally within our budget!"

I opened the wine and poured two glasses into the plastic coffee mugs on the desk. I handed her one as she got on her laptop to show me the Zillow page for what she was sure would become our new Austin home.

I let the cabernet breathe for a few minutes and noted that it actually had a decent aroma. It was just too bad that I was sipping it out of a plastic cup. Maybe I should have bought a $20 Dom's Market wine glass.

I drank a larger than average sip of the wine and noticed one particular flavor that had caught my attention.

Something about it tasted like a cover-up.

CHAPTER 27

I slept well that night, but was woken up by the news that morning reporting that a fireworks gender reveal party on 6th Street in Austin had torn through an outdoor bar and set a busboy's hair on fire.

They were having a girl.

I was having a hard time focusing on this Kinky Friedman project. Luckily, Vreeland sent me a bunch of back information on what we would be discussing and I set off in my car two hours south of Austin towards the tiny town of Medina, Texas, where the legendary singer-songwriter and mystery novelist Kinky Friedman resided on his ranch with six dogs, ten cats and an armadillo.

I had started out early and driven out on I-35 as my wife slept in. The night before we had finished the bottle of Longhorn and spoke to the kids, who had now grown extremely tired of grandma.

"All she does is drink wine and play Words With Friends," my son complained.

There are worse ways to spend your 70's.

Agreeing that I needed a few extra days to see if I could nail down this case, my wife would be driving back alone the day after my visit with Kinky to get the kids and eventually head back to L. A. I had talked her out of putting a down payment on her Austin dream house, but she was dead serious about leaving Los Angeles.

Driving through the Hill Country, Texas is pretty fascinating. The political climate skews very liberal in Austin. Not so much just outside of Austin. Within 10 miles, the Donald Trump flags began appearing. The other thing that began appearing, were the wineries.

I had no idea that an entire stretch of highway in Texas was home to so many gorgeous wineries. I passed places called Dry Heat, Stone Ridge, Pearl Creek and Black Lotus. They boasted of the best peach wine in the world and served meads, reds, whites and rose. Having spent the majority of my adult life as a pretty serious wine drinker, I was ready to blow off Kinky Friedman altogether and settle in for a long afternoon of tasting Texas-bred Malbec. As I made mental notes as to where I would come back to once this whole Casey Dixon thing was behind me, I suddenly recognized a familiar logo on a building up ahead.

Longhorn Creek Estates.

I pulled over to the side of the highway to inspect the area. There was a massive vineyard to the left and a "Welcome Wine Lovers" sign above the open door. It was spacious and massive, three times the size of the wineries I usually frequented off of Dry Creek Valley Road in Healdsburg, California. Everything's bigger in Texas.

I took a few dozen photos of the place and texted Vreeland to get us back in for a tasting the following night. He said he'd have Lindsay do it and I took back off towards Medina with my recording equipment riding shotgun next to me. That's when I noticed that Kinky Friedman had called me and left a voicemail. It began with:

"Rob? Hi Rob - this is Richard Kinky Big Dick Friedman... Let me know what time you'll be coming down and I'm looking forward to having you at the ranch."

Richard. Kinky. Big Dick. Friedman? Man, I had to work on my name when leaving a voicemail.

I called Kinky back - to his landline (he owns no computer or cell

103

phone) around 10:15 AM and he asked me to meet him for lunch at a Jalisco-style restaurant called El Matador in the nearby town of Kerrville. I showed up, met Kinky in the parking lot and watched as nearly ten customers approached him with awe and some sort of story about how they were "past acquaintances."

"Hi Kinky, remember me?" one chipper, maskless gentleman offered. "We did some repair work on that cowboy shirt of yours a few years ago?"

"Yeah, sure. Right," Kinky replied.

"Hi Kinky! Bob Carter. I tended bar In Nashville in the 70's"

"Don't remember ya."

"Hi Kinky. Once I was driving to Austin and you were three cars in front of me and I honked and you looked over and - "

"Let's just take the picture, eh?"

I witnessed first hand what it was like to be one of the kings of Texas.

Kinky asked for chips and salsa at the table at least three times which never seemed to come. When our meals arrived, we ate quickly and settled up to pay the bill. As I reached for the bill, the waiter finally brought us the chips and salsa.

"I think they've got a problem with their sequencing here," Kinky said.

After I paid the bill ($13.00 for huevos rancheros, sweet tea and my tacos - $13.00 won't get you a margarita in Los Angeles), Kinky and I went to the nearby grocery store to buy dog food for his six dogs. As we traipsed through the aisles of the store, life as we know it, in these Covid times, seemed normal again. Barely anybody wore masks. Kids played in the park. Nobody did a head count at the store entrance. It was surreal. Folks in the Hill Country had decided that this virus wasn't worth scaring yourself indoors for the rest of your life and had resumed about as sane an existence as I had witnessed since February, 2020.

Still, this was Texas, and my mom had warned me to 'fit in as best you can' when she heard I'd be going outside of the Austin bubble.

Normally in these types of places, I try to hide my Judaism and talk in some sort of fake southern drawl to fit in with the proud Americans who really want to make our country great again. I'm surprisingly good at southern accents. However this time, I didn't need to use any fake accents. I was hanging out with the most famous Jewish man from Texas in the history of Texas. I felt bulletproof.

After the store, I followed Kinky to his Echo Hill ranch, where he had grown up on a summer campground run by his beloved late parents. His sister Marcie was there to welcome me, and explained that she was preparing the camp for the summer sessions of 2021, if we were lucky enough to be back in a functioning world by then.

The first thing I noticed as I walked into Kinky's home was the smell of the dogs and the cigars, but according to many of Kinky's past novels, he hadn't been able to smell anything since 1981... That made sense. I chuckled to myself about the Billy Joe Shaver bumper sticker plastered on his refrigerator:

"You're only as old as the women you feel. ." - Billy Joe Shaver.

I could go on and on about my night with Kinky, which included shots of Patron Tequila, microwaved Texas gumbo, five cigars, a hilarious interview and discussions about Bob Dylan, the Rolling Thunder review tour, partying in the 1970's, Joni Mitchell, Levon Helm, Rick Danko, Richard Manuel, Dennis Quaid, Nashville, Tompall Glaser, Willie Nelson, Waylon Jennings, marijuana, his past girlfriends, tequila, cocaine and writing. .. But those are other stories for another time.

The only story he truly helped me with was the Casey Dixon murder mystery, which I brought up following what must have been my seventh shot of tequila.

I told Kinky the story of how it all started, the weird communication from Alfie Adams, my arrest, Alfie's death, Mike Porter, the superintendent and finally Tony Valero, Kinky became super engaged and interested in my adventure.

"You know, Rob," he said. "I used to solve a few mysteries myself... Of course I also made them all up in my head for myself to solve."

"Any ideas on where this case is leading, Kinky?" I asked, hoping he had been playing close attention.

"Alfie Adams did it."

"How do you figure?"

Kinky then laid out his theory as to what exactly transpired with the murder of Casey Dixon.

According to his ten-minute knowledge of the case, Kinky surmised that Casey Dixon was pregnant with Mike Porter's baby. Alfie Adams was obsessed with Casey and took it as a personal insult that someone else had impregnated his pretend girlfriend. So, he waited around her apartment spying on her, like he usually did, and saw his opportunity to kill her once I left the building. He said the key to this case was the relationship between Alfie and Mike Porter.

"Or," he said. "The superintendent did it. Wouldn't be the first time that the clues were right in front of your face."

Wow. Kinky's theories were interesting, but I couldn't be convinced so easily. There were still so many unanswered questions, such as:

"How does Tony Valero and Longhorn Creek play into this at all? Why would someone send that email from MY address?"

"I have no fuckin' idea, Rob... You gotta figure that shit out yourself. This case is way too much for me to handle right now. I don't even have email."

I took a final shot of tequila from Kinky's infamous bull horn shot glass and nodded my head. As I went into how I was recording all of this for a true crime podcast, Kinky let me know his thoughts on this popular new form of digital media.

"Podcasting is just another one of those things that will be hot for a while but will one day go the way of the Hula Hoop."

CHAPTER 28

I woke up in Kinky's guest room annex the following morning and shook off the mild tequila hangover. I had recorded Kinky's theories on Casey Dixon into my computer the night before and was listening back to what he had guessed was going on. Smart fucking guy, I thought. I almost had enough here for an entire podcast episode.

Kinky then walked in with a cup of strong black coffee and handed it to me.

"Rob, I was thinking about the murder case you're working on and my sister Marcie reminded me of something this morning," he said.

"Yeah, what?"

"You mentioned Longhorn Creek Vineyard. Well, I've played there before - around 2016. I did an event for my rescue animal charity and I recall meeting this Tony Valero fellow."

"Seriously? What was he like?"

"Fuck if I remember. I just know he let me smoke a cigar in the back office. The thing was, the office was like, tightly sealed - combo locks, high security stuff. Maybe he's hiding some sort of evidence in there."

"We should go there together! Maybe he'll let you in the office and we can look around."

"I'll pass," he said. "I'll let you do the work on this one alone."

I nodded at Kinky and accidentally spilled a drop of coffee on the rug. He didn't seem to notice, or if he did, he didn't care.

"I do remember one other thing," he said. "The back office combo lock passcode is 10012 - Same zip code as I had when I lived in Greenwich Village."

"Wow, thanks man, I'll let you know if it still works."

I said good-bye to Kinky and drove back up through Kerrville. I once again passed by the Longhorn Creek Estates and saw an email on my phone saying that Lindsay had us booked for a wine tasting in their outdoor area at 6:00 that night. I texted her the Greenwich Village zip code and told her not to erase it before calling my wife. I told her I'd bring the car back so she could take off to Tucson and we once again discussed a possible move to Austin.

"What about Medina, Texas?" I asked her.

Driving through these wineries had me considering it...

I pulled back into the Hotel San Joaquin and found my wife packed and ready to go. This little trip to Austin had been the best thing we could have asked for. I wasn't trying to become another marriage fatality of Covid-19. My wife drove off back to my mom's house, promising to stop at the Red Range Inn in Van Horn for the night so she didn't get too tired. I kissed her good-bye.

"You smell terrible," she said.

Some men come home smelling like perfume and lipstick after a long night out. I smelled like dogs and cigars.

"I appreciate that," I replied.

"Think about the house. If we sold our place in L.A. we could easily afford it."

I nodded and walked her out before walking over to Momo's and had my 27th and 28th breakfast tacos of the week. I sat down and thought about Kinky's theory on the case. He did have some great observations. I was hoping some of the stuff would come together at the wine tasting later that night. I lowered my mask and ate the tacos, taking some time to listen to Kinky's music that was available on the Spotify app. For a second I thought about his career. Country rock singer - turned mystery writer/politician. I couldn't help but notice that it somewhat mirrored mine. Country rock singer turned true crime podcaster.

I had only a passing interest in politics.

I went back to the room and recorded some more stuff for the episodes, editing in some of Kinky's music and hoping that he could secure the rights to the song Resurrection for the project. I emailed Lawrence in L. A. and told him how successful the interview had gone and he seemed very happy. Vreeland was pleased too and we met back up at Stereo to have a late lunch before the visit to Longhorn Creek Estates.

Lindsay met up with us for my recap about my night with Kinky. I shared some files with Vreeland from Dropbox and I went over some of Kinky's theories.

"Incredible stuff man," Vreeland said. "I knew he'd have some insight."

The waitress came by with a round of drinks and Lindsay asked why we were starting to drink beer before we got to the winery. I told her that I was riddled with anxiety and needed to take the edge off before visiting the Longhorn Creek Estates. I had already been framed for a murder. I was playing all the angles as best I could. She quickly added a local craft pilsner to the order.

"I'm also going big tonight because my classes got cancelled for tomorrow," Vreeland revealed. "Half the campus tested positive for Covid."

"Frat party?"

"What else."

Lindsay decided that since the winery was 35 minutes out of Austin, that she should be the designated driver. Vreeland and I slammed another beer before we left and took off towards Longhorn Creek Estates around 5:15 PM. The drive was easy, and once we left the friendly confines of Austin proper, the real America started appearing again. Farms, road houses, mom and pop convenience stores. The stuff that was disappearing from every city across our country. Eventually, we pulled up to the enormous gates of the Longhorn Creek and marveled at the sheer size.

"Nice little fixer-upper we got here," Vreeland said.

We parked near a bunch of others, including a group of aging women who belonged to a Johnson City Canasta club. A sign outside of their van read, "Canasta-farians" - which was totally offensive to the Rastafarian religion, but I was sure that at the tender age of 75, these women didn't give a shit about offending anybody. I would have been surprised if any of them even knew what Rastafarian religion even was.

We sat socially distanced apart at picnic tables and the pretty tasting room servers came by with a digital menu for snacks and drinks and of course, a second digital menu for their merchandise. More shirts, corkscrews, masks and bandannas.

"We're having a special on our masks today," Susie, our bubbly server informed us. "They're $15.00 - so five dollars off."

"So the original price is... uhmmm... give me a moment. I'm terrible with math. Uhhhhhh... 20 bucks?"

"You're an idiot, Stoner," Vreeland said. "Bring us the first wine flight and two cheese plates."

As the sun slowly went down on what I imagined was one of the only remaining blue skies in America based on this outbreak of fires we were having in late 2020, it was actually very nice. The wine was terrific, the cheese was perfectly sharp and Lindsay did her best to pour her wine into my glass as a way to stay sober so we could get home and not end up with a DUI on the way home. As clean as the Austin Police Department was, I had no interest in spending any more time there.

"We have to get inside the building," I nudged Vreeland. "Poke around... see what we can find. Just sitting out here is nice, but useless."

"I know but the main tasting room is closed," he said.

"Yes, but you know what's not closed? The GIFT SHOP."

I pointed to the bridge club, and the 11 "Canasta-farians" who had just walked out of it wearing Longhorn Creek t-shirts and masks.

"Bingo," Vreeland said.

"Wrong game," I said. What's the saying you yell when you win a game of Canasta?"

"Uno?"

"Is it?"

We broke out laughing.

"Will you guys make a plan and stop messing around?" Lindsay said.

Lindsay was right. The beer and wine was making me loopy. I had information to gather.

"Lindsay, what was that zip code I texted you earlier?" I asked.

"Uhm... 10012."

I stood up and started observing how the gift shop was set up. This should be an easy operation. I have always been an expert in bypassing security. It had helped me numerous times in previous podcasts, however my specialty was getting backstage at concerts, and NOBODY I had ever met was better at me than doing it. I was a master at forging backstage passes, carrying empty mandolin cases past security guards and dressing like an employee and casually cruising into Comic-Cons, office buildings and festivals. Over the years I had met nearly all of my musical heroes from Willie to Tweedy to both remaining Beatles.

The one time it actually back-fired was when Bruce Springsteen's security guard kicked me out of the final concert ever held at the Los Angeles Sports Arena after he caught me slugging from a bottle of wine in the Boss' dressing room.

I had been in Bruce Springsteen's dressing room. I could get into the Longhorn Creek Estates.

I stood up and asked our server if we were able to enter the gift shop and she said, "mask up!" I employed Vreeland, who was slightly nervous about the entire operation, but agreed to run a bit of a distraction. The plan was to get Vreeland to take an obnoxious amount of shirts and whatever other shit they sold at the register. As the employee added up his order, he would fake a seizure of some sort, fall to the ground and draw the interest of the teenage security guard who had been yawning in the corner for the past 30 minutes. As the crowd converged on Vreeland, I would slip through the roped exit and slide my way into the main tasting room.

I sauntered around the gift shop, asking casual questions like,"Are the magnets heavy sellers?" before Vreeland appeared and began piling up t-shirts at a comical pace. The cashier turned her attention to Vreeland, thinking that this was going to put her over her sales quota for the month. He walked up to the front and placed a large stack of t-shirts in front of the poor young lady, who smiled wide and began running the pricing gun over the tags. Vreeland looked me over and winked before clutching his heart and dropping to the floor.

"Oh my GOD," the young cashier freaked. "Sawyer! Help!"

The teenage security guard left his post and ran over, pulling from an asthma inhaler as he got there. He rolled Vreeland over to his back just as two servers ran in from the outside picnic tables. Nobody was paying any attention to me. I lifted the velvet rope and cruised into the main tasting room with ease, ducking beyond the wine counters and ran into the door of the back office. I saw the combo lock and prayed that Kinky had relayed the right number code to me. I looked around before typing the numbers into the keypad.

The door clicked open and I slid inside. I was suddenly in the same office Kinky had used as a dressing room years earlier, surrounded by bottles of wine, photos of employees and a table with a large desktop computer.

I hit the spacebar of the desktop and it came on. I scanned the framed faces on the wall, trying to see if anyone looked familiar. Whereas none of the employee names rang a bell, one of the names on an "Employee of the Month" plaque did. ..

Engraved beneath the month of April 2018 was the name "MIKE PORTER."

CHAPTER 29

I took a picture of Porter's name with my iphone and recorded some dialogue into my phone about what I was doing. I kept my tone hushed as I did my best amateur computer-hacking on the desktop. Other than my mother-in-law, nobody I knew used a desktop anymore. This was like being back in high school journalism editing my school newspaper on a program called "Layout" or something. It was damn confusing and we often put out newspapers with typos in them.

I wasn't able to get into any emails on the computer, as they were password protected, but I did notice that there was a recently opened Apple Music app that was obviously used to pipe music into the indoor speakers placed all around the tasting room.

I also found a Company Directory folder and opened that.

I typed Mike Porter's name in and found some sort of database of current and former employees. The entire thorough history of the winery was right there. I went down the line, and caught a few recognizable names from my most recent adventure. Alfie Adams, who had been fired for having not disclosed his police record. Casey Dixon, who had been interviewed and denied a job based on past "criminal activity" and Mike Porter, who had been fired for selling fraudulent spirits on the premises.

I had no idea what that meant, but it sounded like it may have something to do with the tampered wine bottles. I wasn't sure, but it seemed like Porter had a nice side hustle going.

In the Apple Music app I found mixes someone had put together entitled "Texas Sippin'" and "Generic Wine Ambience." On the playlists, Guy Clark and some later Steve Earle seemed to be the dominant artists. At the end of the "Texas Sippin'" playlist, I even spotted Sold American by my new pal Kinky Friedman.

I was surprised that they didn't play Ride 'Em Jewboy.

Things got very strange, however, when I clicked on the podcast menu to the left of the player. Normally, someone might listen to podcasts in their cars, at the gym or even while working around the house. I wasn't aware of many wine tasting rooms that played podcasts. But what caught my eye was what I saw was the top podcast on this computer's network.

The Cigarette Girl by yours truly.

Whoever was using this computer had been following me and my content for years. Four of my other podcasts were there too. This guy even downloaded the digital music EP I put out with Night Bears in 2005. Hey, at least I knew where I was getting my listeners from.

Just as I took a picture of the podcast listings, I heard someone typing numbers into the door combo lock. Suddenly, it was kicked in. Directly in front of me stood Sawyer, the teenage security guard, and a man in a broad, Texas suit who was chomping a large cigar. He blew the smoke in my face and I coughed.

"The cigar smoke getting to you, Mr. Stoner?".

"No, I'm actually becoming pretty used to it," I told him.

Behind his suit's shoulder pads, I could see that Vreeland was being restrained in the gift shop by two larger men and a younger member of the Canasta-farians. The crowd of wine-tasters looked inside from the outdoor picnic area.

I glanced down at this imposing man's boots. Gator skin. He had a Longhorn Estates mask on which he removed and hung from his right ear. His slacks were tailored and the belt had been loosened at least twice in the duration of him owning it. I wasn't one to judge. Since Coronavirus shut the gyms down I was back up to a shade below 200 pounds, but luckily, with my shirt off I looked more like 250.

Whatever the case, I was pretty sure I was standing face to face with the one and only Tony Valero.

"Why don't we have a talk, Mr. Stoner. Somewhere away from this crowd."

"I dunno, don't you have some of my podcasts to catch up on?"

"Cute. I don't need to catch up on anything of yours. You already put my half-brother away, I'm just figuring out a way to thank you."

Half-brother? Who was his half-brother? What was happening?

"Tell you what - tomorrow afternoon, why don't you meet me out on Lake Travis? We can take a little boat ride and discuss an idea I have for a podcast. You may like the working title... Austin Translation."

Tony and one of the guys manhandling Vreeland a few feet back started laughing.

"But that's the title of what I'm working on," I pathetically offered.

"Tomorrow. Lake Travis. 1:30 PM. We can fish for our lunch, drink a few glasses of my Pinot Grigio, and also discuss why this podcast you are recording probably WON'T be happening. It'll be nice out, so dress for the warm weather. In the meantime, you and your friends are free to go. Enjoy the Hotel San Joaquin."

I shook myself past him and made it back to the gift shop to find Vreeland and Lindsay who had been ordered to leave the premises as well. The strange thing was that they had roughly fourteen shopping bags with them.

"What's all this stuff?" I inquired.

"They made me buy everything I brought up to the cashier," Vreeland said. "What the hell am I going to do with 35 Longhorn Creek t-shirts?"

I looked over my shoulder and saw Tony Valero staring at me.

I didn't stop talking the entire drive back. I told them about how he had all of my podcasts downloaded on his computer, the fact that Mike Porter had been an employee of the month in 2018 and the weird boat trip planned for the next day. I had a trembling feeling that the adrenaline of this evening was about to send me down a dark spiral of paranoia. I reached into my pocket for my cigarettes. There were four left.

"Don't smoke in here," Lindsay pleaded.

I agreed to hold off and relayed copious verbal notes into my recorder app. We were ten minutes from being back at the Hotel San Joaquin when Vreeland came across a piece of information through a journalism connection he had from college.

"Hey, Stoner - I just reached out to my friend at the Austin Chronicle," he said. "Get this... You know how you said Tony Valero said that you put his half-brother away? Guess who he was."

"Who?"

"Vincent Caggiano," he said as my heart sank to my flip-flops. "The Cigarette Girl Killer."

Vincent Caggiano was the man I had put away with my first true crime podcast all those years ago. I suddenly envisioned myself being cast off of a boat into the depths of Lake Travis, a bullet hole through my chest.

I began to panic.

"Do you know anywhere that sells bulletproof vests?" I asked.

"You mean a life vest?" Vreeland responded.

"No, a bulletproof vest to save my life."

Vreeland sighed.

"So, like I asked... a life vest."

CHAPTER 30

An hour later, my mother-in-law overdosed on THC.

I received a text from my wife as she was lying on her cardboard bed at the Van Horn, Texas Red Range Inn.

My mom is in the hospital, I'm freaking out. Call me.

My mind ran through the usual thoughts. My mother-in-law had a heart attack? A stroke? Or, God forbid... her 250 pound cat attacked her and ate her eyeballs out of her skull?

I called my wife and digested the facts.

"Oh my God," she screamed. "My mom is terrified. She thinks she had a stroke and started thinking weird thoughts and says she has no idea what happened in the last four hours."

"I'm not a doctor, but she sounds super fucking high. What did the doctor say?"

"He said my mom told him that she ate some gummies from our multi-vitamin bottle. Did you put fucking THC gummies in our vitamin bottle or something?"

Uhhhhhhh. Oh.

"Well, genius, my mom ate three of them earlier thinking they were vitamins and thirty minutes later she called 911 claiming that Marge Simpson was dancing in the living room holding a hamster."

"Jesus, it was just marijuana. It's not like it was LSD," I said wrongfully defensive.

"How strong were those gummies? The doctor wants to know."

"I think those were 5 milligrams?"

"Jesus Christ, Rob."

So, my poor 75-year-old mother-in-law, who has been drunk a grand total of ONCE in her entire adult life, gobbled up 15 mgs of THC in one sitting and was now seeing iconic cartoon characters walking around my house.

"I'm so sorry," I said. "I had no idea she would assume she could eat our vitamins." I waited a beat before offering the following, "Also, why would she think that was okay?"

"If my mom dies, I will never forgive you."

"She's gonna be fine… get her an adult coloring book or something."

"Do NOT be an asshole right now!"

"Okay, hear me out… I'm really sorry about this, alright? I have to go, will you keep me posted?"

"Why? What are you doing?"

"Trying to stay calm," I told her. "I think someone's going to kill me tomorrow."

CHAPTER 31

I made my way to my hotel room, again having a full-blown anxiety attack thinking that I had lost another stupid key, and decided to re-listen to my podcast The Cigarette Girl.

As I mentioned earlier, my true crime podcasting career took off when I released The Cigarette Girl through a friend's startup podcast network that was known for celebrity "two microphones and a guest" shows featuring vapid actors and comedians talking about things like MMA and ayahuasca. The Cigarette Girl was an instant success, drawing a million downloads and establishing me as a true crime aficionado in the podcasting space. I became a minor podcast celebrity for a year or so, traveling to conventions, events and enjoying brand sponsorship money to talk about how much I loved my new adjustable mattress and home delivery food service. In reality, I never slept on that mattress and I hated the home delivery food, but reading ads made me a good deal of money and that magic year of 2014 was the true peak of podcasting for my individual brand.

The Cigarette Girl was influenced by an article I had read in a Las Vegas newspaper about a Fremont Street casino owner named Vincent Caggiano who, on the brink of losing his casino to gambling debts, bad investments and an ex-wife, became a suspect in the murder of a young girl who sold cigarettes to patrons on the floor of his Fremont Street establishment. The girl, Rory Burkhead, had apparently been his lover - but when she turned up dead in his business partner Charlie Weinstein's home, the police were perplexed. Until evidence started showing up that Weinstein apparently also owed the whole town and killed the girl as payback for Caggiano blowing all their money. They found a murder weapon in a toolbox at one of Weinstein's car dealerships in Henderson and put together a case that exonerated Caggiano and sent Weinstein to jail for 25 years.

Two years later, I came on board, wondering how the police had missed so much evidence against Caggiano. His cellphone had been tracked to Weisntein's apartment, a hardware store where the murder weapon was purchased and to Burkhead's apartment on the night of her murder. However, since Caggiano was a big police department donor and sponsor of numerous charities and events in town, nobody ever thought he was capable of committing such a heinous crime. As it turns out, he had set up Weinstein with fake text messages from bogus cellphones in Burkhead's name and managed to frame his old partner by planting evidence in his dealership. It didn't help that Weinstein had committed gaming machine fraud early in his Las Vegas tenure and by the time he was arrested, the city was ready to string him up by his magnetic roulette balls.

When Caggiano went down for the crime and Weinstein was released, we held a huge press conference, optioned the rights of the story to Lifetime Television and I decided I would no longer be playing shitty bars with my band as a way to scrape together enough money to pay a bill and ignore 16 others.

I took a second look at the email that Vreeland had shared with me. I was now fully convinced that I had been in his sights for a long time.

There was no chance I could sleep that night. I went back to Dom's Market and bought six Texas pilsners and a bottle of Vaughn-Duffy Cabernet.

There was no fucking way I was drinking any Longhorn Creek Estates.

Back in the room, I drunkenly recorded some updates to the podcast, and said some other gibberish into my recorder that I wouldn't recall saying until early the next morning.

I ended up spilling half the bottle of wine on the bathroom floor. Luckily, I had three Longhorn Creek Estate t-shirts to help clean it up.

CHAPTER 32

It's not every day you wake up thinking you're going to die.

I went through my notes from the night before and listened to a drunk and rambling "Last Will and Testament" that, if I actually did perish that afternoon, would be a pretty embarrassing final vocal performance from a one-time true crime podcaster. It went as follows:

Ohhh boy, I may die tomorrow. If I do, my name is Robert Stephen Stoner and this was caused by a guy named Mike Porter and his uhm - a guy named Tony Valero who owns the Longhorn Estate Creek Estates wine place. They have it in for me because in my podcast The Cigarette Girl I sent Valero's half-brother to prison and got an innocent man released and now they are going to tie rocks to my feet and drop me into the Travis Lake, or Lake Travis, whatever the fuck it's called. I will always love my wife and my kids and my mom and dad and siblings and I'm sorry I never really had a connection to dogs or pets of any sort and I'm sorry that I drank so much wine and I'm sorry that I basically (pause). .. My whole life has been weird since my parents divorced and told each other to fuck off and - OH! Tell Kinky Friedman he can finish this podcast... that would be cool. He totally knows me, we're like homies. And my band the Night Bears is totally bad ass and we should have made it - not fucking Mumford and Sons. Fuck them. Signing off, Robert Stoner. (Uncontrollable laughter followed by. ..) Oh shit. (Unintelligible jibberish). BEEP.

As embarrassed as I was at the sloppiness and carelessness of my midnight diatribe. I did not delete it, thinking that this could be a funny little moment in an episode of my podcast should I happen to live another 24 hours. I called my wife to check on my mother-in-law, who was resting comfortably in the hospital having survived her THC poisoning before noticing a trail of discarded matches on the floor leading towards the front door. I opened it up letting cracks of Texas sunlight blind me in the morning haze. It was like I let God's Flashlight into the room. I stepped outside and immediately felt the immediate sting of the Texas humidity. I looked to the ground where I found a cigarette butt I had somehow smoked the night before during my rolling blackout. I also found my pack of American Spirits on the ground. Anxious to see how many I had smoked, I was surprised to discover that I was left with one final cigarette remaining. .. The LUCKY one. Rather than throw it out, I decided to keep it just in case that dumb college superstition of my youth actually helped me on my boat trip in a few hours. I also looked down to my wrist and noticed that my grandfather's watch was no longer there. A quick search under the bed left me without an answer and I started thinking that it could be anywhere in the Austin vicinity, as I couldn't even remember the last time I had it on my wrist.

I guess I had lived without it for this long, it wasn't going to ruin my day.

I hit Momo's for coffee and called Vreeland, who had some information.

"I called Detective Hernandez," he said. "It took me a few minutes to convince him that this was a good idea, but he actually wants to put together an undercover boat squad to follow you and Tony Valero on the lake today. Apparently Valero's been a nuisance for the police forever. Tax stuff, extortion, false PPP loans. .. but he's like Teflon. They've been trying to get him implicated on something for years."

"Great, so what's the plan?"

"We're all meeting at Stereo."

Detective Hernandez and a crew of young officers in their 20's met us at the outdoor picnic tables dressed like complete fraternity party imbeciles. All four were wearing flip-flops, generic "Keep Austin Weird" tank-tops and hats that said TEXAS. It was like that infamous Rob Lowe hat that he wore that simply said NFL while trying to promote his new show during the Super Bowl on Fox. It was an obvious attempt to blend into a world they knew nothing about, and the Oakley Razorblade sunglasses with the croakies straps did not make them look any less than the cops they were. It reminded me of when undercover "narcs" used to come around my high school wearing t-shirts that said Grunge while the rest of us wore Pearl Jam shirts.

You could spot a narc the minute they started walking through the hallways.

"What the hell are you wearing, Detective?" I asked.

"We're undercover," he said.

"Everybody in here can tell you guys are cops," I said.

"No way. We look like every boat party crew on Lake Travis."

"I hope so, otherwise you're gonna get me killed."

We ordered tacos and prepared for the day's activities. Here's what was going to happen:

Hernandez would be on the lake on a rented houseboat an hour before our scheduled 1:30 p.m. meeting, awaiting Valero's craft to get into the water. I would meet Tony Valero at the dock and start boating out for "lunch." Pretending I was unaware of Valero's connection to Caggiano, I would act as natural as possible, as if I really was looking forward to fishing and sipping wine with two strangers in the middle of a lake. I would have to somehow coax an admission of guilt before Hernandez and his boat cops pulled up and asked for some help with a "fake tow" into the docks. Once tethered, they would raid the ship like rowdy buccaneers and arrest the two men.

Oh, and I would be wearing a wire.

I swallowed the last bite of my chicken taco with nervous anticipation and asked the detectives if I might be able to use the recording on the wire for my podcast about this entire situation. To my surprise they said they'd think about it. First, however, they needed me to cooperate. I reluctantly agreed and FaceTimed my kids.

"Dad, when Covid is over and you're home, can we get a puppy?"

I recalled an old magazine article I once skimmed as a child that claimed that children who grew up with pets grew up to love more fulfilled, happier lives.

I grew up with four pets.

Right now, fulfilled, happy lives didn't mean shit.

CHAPTER 33

The first thing I noticed as I drove up to Lake Travis was that it was a beautiful place to be murdered.

I had seen enough Sopranos episodes to know that an ocean off of the Jersey Shore was a way more disgusting place to meet your demise, and that a pristine lake 30 miles outside of Austin was a much better resting place. I also realized that the lake was much bigger than I thought. This would be a pretty easy place to get away with killing anybody, especially if you made it look like an accident... My anxiety lifted a little bit as I passed multiple properties for sale. I parked at the large estate with a stone entrance similar to the one at Longhorn Creek Estates Winery.

I had the uncomfortable police wire on the inside of my button down shirt and wondered where on the lake Hernandez and his houseboat full of fake party cops were stationed, since they had all set sail 45 minutes earlier. I took a deep breath and walked towards the property before a strange man in a dark sweater and slacks recognized me.

"Mr. Stoner," he said. "Follow me."

He led me around the side of the house to a dock where a souped up Cabin Cruiser sat with its engine running. A young man in a flat-brimmed cowboy hat was busy tying up lines preparing to cast-off the ship. The man was Mike Porter.

"Can you believe this coincidence? We both know Tony Valero, crazy right? !"

Nice try, Porter.

"Another day off from the San Joaquin, huh Mike?" I asked.

"I called in sick... I really wanted to hit the water considering how hot it's been."

Uh-huh. More like you wanted my lifeless body to hit the water. Shit.

I was handed a life jacket and I walked onto the sailboat, admiring how cheesy the LED lights looked wrapping around the inside. The life jacket slightly concealed my hidden microphone, which I was worried would be easily recognized by Porter and/or Valero.

"Oh, don't worry about the life jacket," Mike Porter said. "Unless you're a kid you don't need to wear it while you're on the boat - only in an emergency."

Well, damn. There went that cover up.

I recalled something that my father-in-law, an avid boat and airplane captain, once told me.

"Always know the name of the vessel you are on."

I looked on the back of the boat. Also known as the stern as I had learned from either *Captain Ron* or *Overboard*. Some kind of Kurt Russell jam.

It had been christened the "Nauti Girl."

Oh boy.

I was brought onboard and into a small kitchen area, which was referred to as the 'galley,' shown a toilet which was called a 'head' and told to sit in the 'mess' - which was another name for a small table. I hated boat language. I had actually taken a sailing class in college, thinking it would just be yacht rock afternoons in the sunshine off of the Long Beach pier, but was quickly hit with the harsh reality that sailing was much more like complicated engineering than a Michael McDonald song. I couldn't distinguish between a Lanyard and a Halyard and I didn't care. In fact, I had grown to hate the class - and when I had my final exam, which required a crew of students to sail a craft to Catalina Island 26 miles off of the San Pedro Harbour, I claimed I was seasick and hid, for the duration of the trip, cowering down in the bedroom. Oops, I'm sorry. I meant "the stateroom."

I got a C Minus.

I was waiting for somebody to make contact when Mike Porter finally showed up in the mess with a glass of champagne.

"Tony wanted me to welcome you aboard," he said.

I sniffed the glass, aware of the fact that I could be a target here.

"Haha, don't worry - it's not poison... cheers, bruh!"

He drank up and wiped his mouth. I took a small sip and placed it on the table. Porter seemed uneasy.

"Once we get out on the water, we can talk more. In the meantime, meet us up top for fishing."

I felt the boat begin to move into the water and I followed Mike up the stairs. The deck above the galley was slippery and small, but definitely walkable. I patted my wire to make sure it was still there. As I traveled around the side of the boat towards the fishing area in back I finally spotted the silhouette of an elongated cigar being puffed in the Texas afternoon.

In a dream world, that would have been a cigar in the mouth of Kinky Friedman, ready to sip some tequila - or as he called it "Mexican Mouthwash."

In my reality, it was Tony Valero, in his big, dumb, shoulder pad-heavy Texas suit.

"Ahh, Mr. Stoner. Are you ready to catch your lunch?" assured by the world's lamest Bond villain.

I had never caught my own lunch. I certainly had picked vegetables out of our underperforming home garden that had made it into a salad or two, but fishing for dinner had never been a part of my childhood... especially in Tucson.

"Best bass in Texas swim in this lake," Valero said as I tried to bait my hook, missing the mark nearly every time. "Longmouth, guadalupe, white, striped, you name it."

As we went over a choppy wave, I nervously grabbed for a railing.

"First time on a boat?" he asked.

"Unfortunately, no." I said. "I have a father-in-law who lives on his boat so I've puked over many guard rails before."

"Funny," he said. "Hey Robert, why don't you pop open the wine in the cooler?"

I moved over to the cooler and opened the lid, revealing a decent amount of Longhorn Creek Pinot Grigio, a few beers and a Longhorn branded corkscrew opener. I opened a bottle and poured three glasses before pocketing the corkscrew for protection... Shit, if a wine corkscrew could save my life out here on the somewhat open seas, I'd thank the lord that I never went to rehab when I was 23 like my father had suggested.

Sobriety would have killed me long before this boat trip.

CHAPTER 34

There was a gun in the bathroom.

As I was trying to figure out how to flush the toilet with my foot, I looked over to a shelf full of towels and spotted through a small shelving unit a loaded .22 caliber pistol. It was, as far as Texas guns go, not impressive - but it was still capable of ending a life.

I whispered into my wire. "There's a pistol on board, detective. Repeat, a gun is onboard."

I held the gun in my hand. At first, I considered taking out the ammo so that I would be protected should some showdown come to pass, but I actually have no idea how to remove bullets. I wondered if I should take the gun itself for protection, but figured that would be exactly what they expected me to do. It was too planted. Instead, I hid it beneath a towel and prayed I wouldn't have to use it.

I left a recorded recap of the journey thus far into my phone, knowing I had the wire on for backup and added some humorous vignettes, including what could be the first line of a new song I was thinking of calling "Pistol in the Bathroom." Wow, I hadn't even thought about writing a song in years. Maybe impending doom is a good muse.

So far this boat trip isn't going well... it's called the Nauti Girl, and I've been told that boats with punny names should never be trusted. Oh, and I have a song idea. (Singing) "There's a pistol in the bathroom and the champagne stinks/You'd think a winemaker would serve better drinks..." That's all I got so far. (deep breath).

I climbed back up to the fishing deck. In the time I had been downstairs, Tony Valero had caught three bass. "After we eat, we can talk," Tony said.

From the corner of my eye I swore I saw Detective Hernandez and his undercover houseboat party cruising by. Thank God, I had my back up. .. At closer glance, however, it turned out to be a bunch of shirtless dudes and female influencers in the wild. Unless Detective Hernandez was blataqntly parading his shaved torso and slamming cans of White Claw Seltzer.

"Idiots," Valero said. "This used to be a family-friendly lake but the party kids always ruin it towards the end of the summer."

"Yeah, I get it," I said. "That's like a 'Covid-Boat'"

That got a chuckle out of Valero.

"I've always admired your sense of humor," he said.

Mike fired up a little metal bar-be-cue and began gutting the fish. I finished my wine and poured another. My day-drinking intake reminded me of that terrific Leonardo DiCaprio/Jordan Belfort quote on his doomed yacht in the film The Wolf of Wall Street.

"I will not die sober!"

My phone lost service, which was not comforting. I worried about my wife and my kids and how they were doing now that she had most likely picked them up at Grandma's to get back to L. A. I hadn't been away from my family for this long in a while. Spells without seeing my children was one of the reasons I hated traveling to other cities to do true crime podcasts. When the kids were younger, it was easy to disappear for a couple weeks and miss out on some diaper changing. Now I really needed to be there to help.

"Do you know who created Lake Travis, Mr. Stoner?" Valero asked me.

"Not at all."

"Lyndon Baines Johnson himself. Well, he had help, but... LBJ made all this happen. Did you know that LBJ was from Johnson City just over a few miles from my winery? They named that little town after LBJ's great uncle. Anyway, when LBJ was in office, he actually paid an architect to rebuild an exact replica of his Texas childhood home for visitors to come visit. Can you imagine that? Having an ego so big that you think that Americans are going to want to see what the house you grew up in looked like? I grew up in a six floor walk-up in Manhattan. Nobody wants to visit MY family apartment."

I bet I knew the zip code.

"Why are you telling me this?" I asked.

He took a draw from his cigar and tapped ash into the lake.

"Men who think they're revealing important things that draw attention to themselves often aren't aware of the other people's lives they are messing with."

I was starting to think I knew what Valero was hinting at. Was he making a terrible reference to the fact that I had become a successful podcaster at the expense of his half-brother? I wasn't following his train of thought but thus far, I was just trying to stay on my toes.

"Well, Mr. Valero: if it helps, I've seen Nixon's birth home; Monticello, Mount Vernon; and TI's Trap House Museum."

"What the hell is a 'Trap House Museum?'"

"Check it out next time you're in Atlanta."

An hour later, we were eating the bass at a plastic folding table out the bow or the stern of the ship. The food was actually delicious although it needed lemon and hot sauce and I thanked the lord that it was any type of food other than a taco.

As Mike told a story about how he once landed a 200 pound tuna, I tuned out, noticing that Valero was as bored as I was. And then my hidden wire began feedbacking.

Thinking fast, I went to a far corner of the boat and tried to figure out why it was short-circuiting. I was in full blown panic mode, convinced that Valero had heard the feedback and was sharpening his fish slicer as I pretended to enjoy the view of the lake. With no other options, and unable to get the wire to turn off, I decided to throw it overboard. It hit the water and floated on the surface for a few seconds before circling and dropping to the bottom of the lake.

I was sure I'd be joining it down there momentarily.

Valero directed the boat to a far north corner of the lake. There were two older houses that hadn't been tended to in some time rotting on a small patch of land near a thick underbrush of trees. We finished our food and Mike poured more wine.

And then the man in the dark sweater - who had met me at the front of Vaelro's house earlier - popped up from below deck and began strangling Mike Porter.

I jumped backwards and knocked my wine glass to the floor. As Mike struggled, the man in the dark sweater tightened his grip around his neck. Mike kicked his legs helplessly and I finally mustered the courage to speak.

"What the hell are you doing to him?"

I wasn't sure what to say. I wanted to alert Detective Hernandez. I was scared. Mike's face was turning red. This shit was real. Finally, the man in the dark sweater let him go. He crawled over to me as I gently gripped the wine corkscrew in my pocket.

"Well well well," Valero said. "Mr. Porter, how do you feel about our little boat trip now?"

"What the FUCK, Tony!" Mike gasped.

Tony slapped Mike pretty hard.

"You had ONE JOB!" he yelled. "One simple job…"

Something strange was happening here. I thought Mike would have been in on this all along, having been brought on board to kill me. Apparently, he was just another murder target in Valero's telescopic sight.

Mike was bent at the waist and struggling to find air.

"How was I supposed to know that Rob would reject Casey's advances?! Name ONE man in the world who could have said no to Casey!"

"I will name one man..." Valero said. "His name is Rob Stoner."

In a dumb comedy film I would have waved at Mike and eeked out a wry smile. Instead, I chose to keep my hands low.

"Also," Valero continued, "What kind of fucking idiot sends an EMAIL to the man who has HIRED HIM to kill someone?"

"I didn't know you could find out who was 'blind copied' in an email! You have to believe me," Mike pleaded. "How did I know they would even look into that?"

Even I knew that was a stupid answer.

The smack of a wooden oar against a man's head is not something I recommend hearing. Mike went down hard. As the man in the dark sweater came towards me brandishing the oar, I began yelling "help" as loud as I could... The last thing I saw was the butt of an oar coming at me like I was a fastball in Aaron Judge's wheelhouse.

Everything went black.

CHAPTER 35

I woke up 45 minutes later, my head pounding. I saw two of everything, including Tony Valero, who was using the same wine corkscrew I had stolen earlier from his cooler to open another bottle of Pinot Grigio.

"Good morning, Mr. Stoner. Don't worry, it only hurts for about an hour."

I took a minute to get my bearings and realized that Mike was still out cold, tied up to the plastic deck chair a few feet away. Around his hands were multiple lines of familiar looking rope.

Yellow polypropylene rope.

Valero paced in front of me.

"So… you were trying to steal my wine corkscrew? Do tell - why? We sell them in our gift shop at the Longhorn Winery. Surely you could have splurged the twelve bucks last night."

"I liked your graphic designer. What do you want from me?"

As I was slurring through my words and wondering where the hell Detective Hernandez and his party boat was, I reached into my pocket and pressed record on my phone app. If I was going to ever survive this, I wanted it all in the Cloud. Maybe my kids would one day think that their father was a brave badass, and not just the guy who shrieked like a five-year-old when a rabid squirrel ran through our kitchen once.

In my defense, it was a big fucking squirrel.

"Let me ask you a question, Mr. Stoner. Do you enjoy wrecking families?" Tony Valero asked.

"What? No! What are you talking about?"

"My half-brother. Vincent Caggiano."

"Name sounds familiar - "

"Don't pretend you don't know. You were responsible for putting him away for 50 years. Which means my mother will never see her little baby boy again."

"Well, what about that cigarette girl he murdered? What about her parents?"

"Who cares? Some midwestern bar slut is dead, and nobody bats an eye. An Italian businessman who was employing over 5,000 people goes to jail, lives are ruined. .. Do you follow me?"

"On Twitter? No."

He looked at me. Was he holding back a laugh? I couldn't tell. But he took his anger out on Mike Porter, kicking his chair against the side sending the whole package down to the deck once again.

"I recognize that rope you tied him up with... Polypropylene?"

"Indeed it is. Did your father-in-law teach you that on his boat, Mr. Stoner?"

"Not really, that's just the same type of rope that was used to strangle Casey Dixon," I said, assuming that Detective Hernandez had given up. I began to think I shouldn't have tossed my hidden microphone into the lake.

"That's a very astute observation," He said. "You should have been a private investigator - like my friend here."

He pointed to the man in the dark sweater.

"You're a private investigator?" I asked.

"One of the best in Texas," Valero said. "Also was a button man in New York before I moved him out here. Been trailing you since you got to town... Let me ask you a question, Robert. Did you notice him?"

"Not at all. What the hell is a button man?"

"Someone who fucking kills people."

I peed myself a little.

"Shit - this was all supposed to be so simple. You and Casey were gonna go to her apartment, you get naked and then Mike was gonna come in and kill you both. .. Unfortunately, your honor and commitment was not what I expected from a failed musician who is most likely going through a midlife crisis."

"I don't understand."

Valero laughed and re-lit his cigar. He went above the flame. Like Kinky Friedman did.

I slid back on the deck and reached into my pants and took out that pack of American Spirits. Valero watched as I calmly flipped open the top. One cigarette remained. The LUCKY.

"Sorry, Mr. Valero - Do you mind if I smoke this on the boat? Since you're gonna kill me and all? It's my final cigarette ever."

Valero laughed for a moment before lighting my cigarette.

"It's too bad you had to fuck with my family, Stoner. I kinda like you."

I took a deep pull off of the LUCKY cigarette and recalled the great Bruce Springsteen lyric:

When it comes to luck, you make your own.

I exhaled and thanked Tony Valero for the light. Like most guilty egomaniac narcissists that I seem to interview in my podcasts, Valero continued telling me more and more information about the murder.

"Casey Dixon, the young girl who was murdered - she was pregnant - were you aware of that?"

"Yeah, I knew that... I always assumed it was Mike Porter's baby."

He laughed extremely hard at that one. "Hahahahaha."

"What's so funny?" I asked.

"Mike Porter? MIKE PORTER? Please, this fuckface couldn't get a girl like Casey Dixon in his wildest dreams! I was the one sleeping with Casey... That was MY baby. Jesus Christ! You hadn't figured that out yet? Maybe your detective skills DO suck."

I've never claimed to be a private detective. Just a podcaster. If I had been forced to hunt down killers in the pre-internet days I would have sucked at my job. I'm pretty much a scared little boy who still jumps at loud noises and has anxiety attacks whenever a strange sound echoes through my house in the middle of the night. I am what is known as an internet sleuth and in no way have I ever claimed to fit in with the bad ass private dicks of the world. Most clues and hunches I follow are straight out of Google search engines.

Still, I had to prod Tony Valero just a little further.

"Here's my question, Valero: You were sleeping with Casey?" I asked. "Why did you have her try to seduce me?"

He smirked just as Mike Porter started somewhat coming back to life in his plastic chair. Valero took a long look out over Lake Travis and exhaled a puff of cigar smoke. A speedboat raced by with a waterskiing fraternity brother doing his best to make rooster tails behind it.

"This all comes down to Mike Porter, Mr. Stoner," Valero said. "Mike owed me money. A lot of money, actually. He had used my wine labels to scam a bunch of wine investors - that kind of thing... Long story, but he tarnished my brand by basically selling shiner wines in my labels for fifty bucks a bottle.

Those must have been the bottles they sent to Vreeland and the UT Journalism Department.

"Since Porter here still owed me a bunch of money, I sent him to kill Casey... And to frame you. You screwed up my family? I'm screwing up yours."

We both exhaled at the same time, our plumes crossing streams.

"We're both happily married men, aren't we Mr. Stoner?" he said. "After all, I know your wife doesn't know what really happened that night with Casey... or does she?"

"I haven't told my wife anything." I lied.

"I figured you hadn't."

He paced back and forth for about 10 seconds. His hands reached for something in his pocket. A pistol? More rope? I was convinced that this was the end.

"By the way, I have a quick question," he stated. "Where did you get this?"

Valero reached down and pulled out my grandfather's watch."

"What? How? How did you get that?" I mumbled.

"Found it in the back office at Longhorn Creek. It must have slipped off your wrist when you were breaking and entering into our private property."

"I didn't break and enter anything, I was just doing research."

Valero laughed. He took my grandfather's watch and held it over the side of the boat.

"Say good-bye," he said, holding it for much longer than I thought he would hold it for.

"Just drop it," I said. "I don't even care anymore."

Amazingly, he did. My grandfather's silver and turquoise watch sank to the bottom of Lake Travis and I said good-bye to it for the second time in my life. .

"Your lack of compassion is somewhat disturbing," Valero said.

"My grandpa has been dead for 20 years," I said.

Suddenly, Valero violently kicked the side railing of the boat. He was pissed off.

"What's wrong?" I prodded.

"This fucking idiot Porter! All I wanted was for him to sneak into your room when you were gone, send that email about the murder-suicide to Austin PD, and that would be enough to put this whole motherfucking thing to bed - INSTEAD, this dumb motherfucker blind-copied my email on it as well for no sane fucking reason…"

Valero kicked Mike's shoulder again. Mike groaned in pain.

"Fucking idiot!" He continued, ashing his cigar on his head in the process.

"Yeah, but what about Casey Dixon?" I asked. "How does she play into it? You killed her over your love child?"

He laughed one of those slow, sinister laughs that never seem to end well for either party.

"Well, Rob… In the old days, Casey is what we would have called a 'paid escort.' Nowadays, this young generation calls them 'influencers' or something. For the right amount of money, they'll do anything you ask. Pose naked, promote your business… Even seduce - or influence - a mark like yourself."

"You're saying that you paid Casey to seduce me?" I asked.

Valero laughed before spewing forth cigar smoke.

"Are you kidding? Of course I did! You think a girl like that is taking home a 45-year-old married guy from the Hotel San Joaquin without some guaranteed cash behind her intentions?"

That stung. To the left of me, the button man laughed and shook his head.

I guess this fact hurt so badly because somewhere, in a long-suppressed dark part of my soul, I was hoping all this time that Casey was into me because, you know, maybe I still had "a little game."

In reality, I was like a customer at a strip club thinking that Bambi the exotic dancer just really liked talking to me.

CHAPTER 36

At my bachelor party in 2005, my buddy Eric had arranged a Las Vegas sushi dinner for me and 10 friends. The catch was, we would be slurping yellowtail off of a naked Japanese girl like we were Yakuza gang members. The practice of eating sushi from a nude woman lying on a dinner table was known as "Nyotaimori" and has since been banned in most countries. (Not due to Covid-19 concerns, but due to the fact that it is a highly degrading and objectifying act).

The plan was that one-by-one we would hoover sushi off of this poor young lady - who looked like she was awaiting a postmortem at the morgue - and then at the end of the meal, as the groom-to-be, I was going to have to lick a bunch of Sake off of her inner thighs. After that, every member of the bachelor party could place Sake anywhere they wanted to on her body and lick it off. For an extra 50 dollars you could rub wasabi on her nipples. Once all the sushi was finished, she would be free to stand up and join us for drinks while dancing naked in the back room of our own private sushi bar.

This made me very uncomfortable. After a spicy tuna roll I tried to eat off of her forearm fell out of my mouth and onto the floor, I decided to leave my friends to go drink alone in the casino bar. Eric was pissed, being that he had dropped $4500 dollars for all of us to feast off of the naked "sushi model" - but even back then I guess I was afraid of things that seemed "too easy."

In a strange way, Casey presented herself to me in a similar way. Not that she was naked and covered in baked salmon rolls, but that she seemed a little too interested in me for it to feel real.

I told Valero this story as if it was my final confession on my deathbed.

Valero suppressed a cough and scratched his nose.

"You really are a pussy," he said."And somehow you turned out to be the only middle-aged man on Earth who says no to a hot bartender who wants to ball your brains out.".

"Yeah, well... I love my wife," I said.

Valero and the button man in the dark sweater both glanced at each other. It made me feel uneasy and unsafe. I tapped my cigarette.

"Bottom line is, Roberto - you messed up our plan - and Mike here is the one who is going to suffer for it. .. Oh, and you're gonna suffer too. I just wasn't expecting to kill two men when this thing started, but you know, I feel a little lost here. Like the title of your podcast you're trying to make... I'm just 'Austin Translation.'"

The button man in the dark sweater approached Mike Porter once again and I began sweating. I watched as he took the same fishing knife that Mike had been using on the bass earlier and began pressing it against that one artery in his neck that I can never spell or pronounce.

Carrororitd?

Carrot?

Convoluted?

"Roughly 29 people die on this lake every year," Valero said. "Looks like this year we can add two more freak water-skiing accidents."

Valero gave a signal to the button man and he put the fishing knife away. Valero picked up the oar and raised it high above his head as he stood over Mike.

And just as I was about to watch a man get killed in front of me, I suddenly remembered the .22 pistol I had hidden beneath the towels in the bathroom.

I jumped up, barely gathering my balance, and tried to run to the stairs to head below deck. Valero watched as I made it exactly two feet before my tied up feet stumbled again and I crashed face first into the deck.

Luckily, that was the exact same time that Detective Hernandez and the other deputies boarded the ship and startled the murderous crew.

Hernandez's voice sounded a lot better this time than the last time I was in the vicinity when he had arrested somebody.

"Tony Valero! Austin Police! Drop the oar and put your hands up!"

CHAPTER 37

Following the seizure of the Nauti Girl and the arrests of everybody else on board, I went to sleep for a long time. When I woke up in my hotel room, it was 8:30 at night and I texted Vreeland and Lindsay to meet me in the Hotel San Joaquin lounge. They swung by. If there was ever a time during this pandemic where I wanted to take my mask off and hug somebody this was it. Instead, we bumped elbows and ordered drinks.

"Holy. Shit." I announced.

"We saw everything on the Austin PD Instagram account," Vreeland announced. "Can we please go big tonight?"

"I'll do my best," I said.

We removed our masks and I told them the whole story, from top to bottom. It was essentially what I planned to make my next true crime podcast about the unfortunate murder of the "Hotel San Joaquin Beauty" Casey Dixon.

Tony Valero's half-brother Vincent Caggiano was a man that I had brought to justice through the Cigarette Girl. Ever since the conviction, Tony had followed my whereabouts, going so far as to hire a private investigator and former contract killer to track me. When I came to Austin to meet with Vreeland and the UT journalism department, I stayed at the Hotel San Joaquin where the manager Mike Porter worked. .. Coincidentally, Valero had once employed Porter at his Hill Country Longhorn Estates Winery (Employee of the month April 2018) until he was fired for selling falsely labeled wine under the nose of the boss and ultimately owing Valero around 25K. To excuse his debt, Valero offered Porter $10,000 to get Casey to seduce me and take me to her apartment while he turned off the Hotel San Joaquin security cameras. Casey's friends had said that in the days leading up to her murder, she had been flashing a lot of cash, which meant that she had been paid for her participation as well. (Remember how much cash she had in that Sparkletts jar?) Once I was out of my hotel room and off the property, Mike would sneak into my room and send a confessional email to the police from my computer before driving over to kill the both of us.

Assuming that Casey and I were going to be locked in the throes of extramarital passion, Mike planned on killing us, setting the scene up to look like I had done the deed myself as a way to escape my marital "infidelities" and the case would be closed, Porter's debt would be paid off and Valero's illegitimate love child and girlfriend would be dead - alongside yours truly.

Mike Porter fucked up by blind-copying Valero to the email he sent to the Austin Police.

I diverted the plan by unexpectedly denying Casey's advances.

According to my case outline, Porter showed up at Casey's apartment around 2:45 a.m. to kill both of us - When I wasn't there, they had some sort of fight and he strangled her with the propylene rope from Valero's boat before taking some of her underwear and planting it in the superintendent's room.

Meanwhile, my old pal Alfie Adams was simply a true crime fan who was obsessed with Casey and was beginning to uncover the affair Casey was having with Tony Valero. Whether or not he was killed or just OD'd would remain a mystery for now.

So, Valero, Mike Porter and the button man in the dark sweater were in jail.

Casey Dixon, her unborn child and Alfie Adams were dead.

And I was five beers in with Vreeland and Lindsay relaying the entire story. When I had finished playing a few recordings of podcast notes I had put into my phone throughout the entire ordeal, Vreeland's face lit up.

"I'm going to say right now that this podcast needs to be on the UT platform - It's a perfect follow-up to The Lemon Grove podcast," Vreeland said.

"Well, let me see what Lawrence and DETAIL says," I said. "Couldn't hurt if you called him and told me how this whole ordeal went down."

"Done deal," Vreeland said. "Lindsay, you're gonna be executive producing this with Stoner."

CHAPTER 38

I woke up the next morning with a call from Detective Hernandez.

"This was a pretty crazy month, Mr. Stoner," the Detective said."First of all, that photo of the footprint that you took in your bathroom matched Mike Porter's boots."

"I told you to look into that last week," I said.

"Yeah, well, it also turns out Mike Porter embezzled something like twenty-five grand from Longhorn Creek Estates when he worked there, using cheap counterfeit wine and the Longhorn Creek label. Have you ever heard of a guy named Rudy Kurniawin?"

Of course I had. Rudy Kurniawan was a master wine forger who sold the billionaires of the world bogus wine in repurposed bottles. The dude was a genius, scamming folks who had claimed to have perfect palates with similar tasting blends, other ingredients and a high resolution label maker. He did it all from the basement of his mother's house before the police raided him and shut down his multi-million dollar fake wine business. I'm pretty sure he's still doing time in a Pecos, Texas prison.

"Porter was an amateur version of Rudy Kurniawan. Valero found out about the scam and fired him, but basically has been extorting him for the past two years. The deal with you was going to wipe out his debt."

"Yeah, I knew that four days ago. What happened to the superintendent?"

There was a long break of silence.

"We released him last night. He said he wanted to get in touch with you and thank you in person."

"Absolutely," I chimed, knowing that an interview with a SECOND man wrongly accused of murdering Casey Dixon would be an unreal addition to the podcast.

"Listen… Robert, I'm so sorry. I just wanted to say that… I'm fairly sure that snake lawyer Mandelbaum is going to try to get you and the superintendent to press charges against us for this false arrest. Any chance you can talk him down from that? We don't need that kind of press right now, especially since police across the country are going through enough as it is."

I took a deep breath and sat back on my bed realizing I still owed Mandelbaum five thousand dollars.

"Hey, detective? As far as I'm concerned you saved my life yesterday. That accounts for something."

"Thank you, Mr. Stoner. That means a lot."

"One question: why did it take you so long to come save my ass on the boat? Didn't you hear all you needed on my mic wire? About the gun in the bathroom and when I got knocked the fuck out by that oar?"

"In this line of work, we like to take it to the last moment of desperation. Last thing we needed here was a third wrongful arrest if that make sense."

"Sounds like the department is doing great," I said.

"Yeah, well… if you're interested, I do have some new information on the death of Alfie Adams."

I hit record on my laptop Blue Snowball microphone and put the detective on speaker phone.

"Go ahead," I said.

"Turns out this guy was stalking Casey Dixon for years. He found out about the affair between her and Valero and then overdosed on Xanax and Fentanyl. At first we thought it was accidental because we didn't know where the Fentanyl came from, but when we arrested Valero, we found some in his car. I'm not saying he killed Alfie, but there's a good chance he had something to do with it. Sorry about that, I know you two were friends."

"Yeah, yeah - that all makes sense."

"Also, Valero had been stalking you for the past 32 months. On his computers we found your home address, names of your kids, where they went to school before the pandemic hit, your mom's address, everything. It's pretty lucky that you're alive right now."

"Wow, that's scary stuff," I said. "Can you help me get a new identity and move my family across the country?"

Detective Hernandez laughed.

"Wrong department," he said.

After recording some updates and notes into my microphone, I booked a 9: 20 p. m. flight out of San Antonio to LAX because it was $185 cheaper than leaving from Austin and I was still awaiting Lawrence's phone call that would put me back on the team payroll. I also decided to fly out of San Antonio because it was way closer to Medina than Austin was and I still had to relay this entire story to one more person before I split town.

I called a familiar phone number and got the answering machine.

"Hello, this is Richard Kinky 'Big Dick' Friedman..."

I left Kinky a voicemail and went to check out.

Before I left the room, I took every branded item that the Hotel San Joaquin offered. A lighter, a couple of matchbooks, a wine corkscrew, a towel, a few soaps and mini shampoos and I even dropped another $15.00 on the ridiculous 1970's keychain.

I wanted stuff to remember this place by.

I finally had all the merch that I needed.

As I rolled my suitcase through the gravelly outdoor halls, I pushed open the side gate and noticed that just behind the daily pool patrons, there was a large Latino man standing in the lounge smiling and waving at me. I was pretty sure it was Roberto Arenas, the superintendent.

"Hello Mr. Stoner? I am Roberto Arenas - thank you for saving my life," he said.

Roberto looked as if he had been violently starved in prison for a week and a half while I was uncovering the facts of the case. I felt so badly for him. I also thought it funny that I had now been associated with three "Roberts" or "Robertos" in this ordeal. Mandelbaum, Arenas and myself.

"If it's OK with you, I'd like to take you to lunch," he said. "I know a good bar-be-cue spot that nobody else knows about - Called "The Pick-Up Pit." The pitmaster cooks the meat in the bed of an old 1976 Ford Ranger Pickup Truck..."

"Why don't we just go get some tacos," I said. "My treat."

"Whatever you want, Mr. Stoner."

Our lunch together was pretty uneventful, other than the fact that Arenas drank five Modelo beers in under 40 minutes. As he sucked down each bottle, like any man who recently dodged a life sentence in prison should, I managed to get him to go on record about how he thought he was framed for the crime.

"I haven't locked my door in 22 years as the super of my building," He explained. "Everybody knew that. I helped people with building issues, problems, anything. And let me tell you, Casey Dixon was a sweet girl who just got mixed up with the wrong guys. She used to come over and tell me how Porter and Valero were basically abusing her mentally, but made sure that she was financially secure. "

"Didn't you do handyman work at Longhorn Creek Estates?" I asked.

"Yessir," he said. "I knew Mike Porter, Valero, all those guys. They knew that I kept my door open so maybe they planted the evidence that night."

"Man, I'm so sorry you had to go through this," I said.

"Thanks. Still? I don't know how I didn't hear Porter sneak into my apartment at three in the morning."

"Real G's move in silence like LASAGNA," I said, quoting Lil Wayne.

"What the fuck does that mean?" he asked.

"Don't worry about it."

I paid for our food and beers and wished Mr. Arenas well before taking my rental car back down towards Medina. On the road, Kinky Friedman called me back and we met back up at the el Matador Restaurant in Kerrville for one final dose of local Mexican food.

This time, I ordered the huevos rancheros.

"Good choice, brother," Kinky said.

I told him the outcome of the case and how his old Greenwich Village area code was key to helping me figure some information out. We discussed how his original thoughts weren't that far off... other than the fact that he suspected Alfie Adams.

"Shit - who knew that the criminal behind this was the rich wine guy - maybe I'm losing a step. I can barely nuke a fuckin Texas Gumbo in the microwave anymore."

The same folks from our first lunch walked up and thanked him for his years of creative contributions to society and Kinky and I discussed my close call with death and how I was almost marooned at the bottom of Lake Travis. His one takeaway from the experience was -

"Shit, man, I've never been hit by an oar. Does it hurt?"

I pointed to the large red welt currently decorating the right half of my face.

"Yeah, ouch. But for a guy like me, that might be an improvement," Kinky said.

Having spent the past week binge watching Kinky Friedman music videos and reading his books, I was sad to be leaving him, but feeling more inspired than I'd been in a very long time. The air of loneliness sort of hangs over Kinky's head, possibly from the lack of international praise that all of his contemporaries have received for their groundbreaking 70's Outlaw Country music or possibly for the lack of a wife or children to call his own. At 76, the man has one of the sharper and quotable minds of anybody I have ever met, an incredible career that brought diversity to the Grand Ole Opry before anybody else and a fading star that deserves to be honored, polished and celebrated not only for his musical accomplishments but for his literary ones as well.

Still, down here, hours from the US/Mexico border - there are very few people around his private ranch to test his material on. That being said, I felt a connection with Kinky that went beyond being country-singers-turned-crime-solvers. It was a sense of familiar camaraderie. A deeper bond that revealed to me the type of man I would have probably grown up to be like had I never fallen in love with my wife and had children. Or, if I had even decided to take it a step further with Casey Dixon on that fateful night two weeks earlier.

"Kinky, why didn't you ever get married? ' I asked him.

"Well, there were a lot of girlfriends," he said. "But the one that truly got away was this Philipino cocktail waitress."

I nodded my head as the waiter once again delivered the salsa and chips after we had finished our main course.

This time, Kinky picked up the tab and invited me back to visit his Echo Hill Ranch any time I felt like it. I thanked him, told him I'd be back as soon as I could and said I might be asking him for some of his music to use in the podcast. He smiled, lit another cigar and said:

"You never know, Stoner, maybe we have something here."

"I think we do," I said.

He got into his truck and drove away.

My next stop was the San Antonio airport.

CHAPTER 39

I returned the rental car, put on gloves, the face masks and the N-95 and once again boarded a fairly packed plane. I refused the beverage service and snacks, pausing only to accept a disinfecting wipe and listened back to my notes from the podcast convinced that I had enough material to possibly win an Academy Award... Or a "Golden Mic" or a "Poddy" or whatever their suggested Oscar-like award show for podcasts was set to be called.

The world needs more award shows like I needed more tacos after this Texas journey.

Come to think of it, at the very least, I might have a chance at winning a "Streamy."

I landed in Los Angeles and took an Uber home.

Checking my emails on my phone once I landed, I was pleased to see that Lawrence had reached out from DETAIL and told me that he would like to hear my podcast on this entire subject before I just gave it away to the UT staff. .. I wrote him back and asked if this meant I still had a job. YES he responded. Just finish this podcast and get it to me ASAP.

I called Vreeland for a final wrap up and he was sadly, under the weather when he answered.

"Vreeland? What's wrong?" I asked.

"The night you left, Lindsay and I went big at a local bar with some students," he said. "I tested positive for Covid-19, but my symptoms are not feverish but I can't taste anything and I'm coughing like crazy."

"Oh my God dude! Are you okay?"

"Well, I guess, but my wife isn't thrilled. I'll be staying at the Volkswagen Touareg for a couple of weeks."

"I understand," I said. "How's Lindsay?"

"Not a symptom. Completely negative."

"Of course. Stay strong, get well and keep me posted OK man?" I offered. "Love you my friend."

"Love you too, Stoner - Can't wait for you to come back."

After I hung up, I realized that NOT EVERYBODY in this world had Coronavirus. Some folks have the immune systems of cheetahs or falcons and can shake off any disease that comes their way... like Lindsay Wi. If this was truly some factory-made disease created to "thin the herd" I wondered why some people were affected so much more than others. For instance, I had been around Vreeland and Lindsay all week. I had flown twice. I was out at multiple bars and restaurants. .. Why didn't I have this thing yet?

And how did Lindsay avoid it?

Whatever the case, I had a new outlook on life. I was done with booze for a while, I had been going pretty hard since quarantine and I figured it was time to chill out and take some time off. Sobriety would give me a chance to focus and edit my new project together in the proper manner.

Arriving home and hoping to surprise my family with another out-of-nowhere surprise appearance, I snuck around the back gate once again and found my son on his latest device, gaming. As I walked up to him he flipped up the mute button on his headphones and greeted me with traditional 14-year-old boy stuck in a global pandemic enthusiasm.

"Hey," he said.

"Hey dude, you good?"

"Not really. Mom won't let me 'Postmates' Chick-Fil-A."

"You know what? Just do it... blame it on me," I said, feeling positive and inspired, like something, anything brilliant was about to come down my path.

"Thanks, dad!" He responded. "What's your credit card number?"

I texted it to his phone and drank a large bottle of water from the pantry.

As I waltzed through the house, kissing my daughter and eventually finding my wife, I noticed how great everything in the house looked, how much the old broken shelves and gates had been fixed and just how magical this small home where I was lucky enough to be spending my adult years was. I found my wife in the hallway and gently tapped her on the shoulder. She turned around and lit up. I kissed her, telling her how much I had missed our family, how much I loved her and how great the house looked. I told her about my podcast, the way I had almost met my death on a powerboat at the hands of a vicious revenge-seeking relative of Vincent Caggiano's and how I had just been given my job back at DETAIL.

After noting how great it was that she had managed to fix the broken sink disposal, the loose floorboards and the broken fence slats, I rubbed her shoulders and thanked her for taking care of all that stuff while I was gone.

She poured herself a glass of wine and sat back on her chair as I playfully wrestled my daughter.

"Don't thank me," she said. "Thank Paul - he was here all weekend."

Oh shit. Paul? I hadn't been checking the Ring app.

"I'm just kidding," she said. "Actually, my dad came by and helped us out... After my mom nearly OD'd on your THC gummies, we needed a 'guide' to talk her down. .. By the way? She broke our ice machine. And she swore that we have a ghost in this house."

We kissed again and I told her how much I looked forward to growing old with her and how I couldn't wait to laugh about all of our wonderful times together while entertaining as many people as we could on whatever property we ended up on after this pandemic. Austin? Northern California? New York? I didn't care. As the helicopters circled our house, spraying lights down towards the realities of the world beyond our bullshit, she kissed me back and held my hand as I smiled as wide of a smile as I have in all the years since we had been married.

"'I'm done traveling for podcasts," I said. "This Austin one could be a game changer and at this point, I just want to be home with you and the kids."

"Well, maybe home can be in Austin," she said. "Melissa is hooking me up with her real estate agent."

"Yeah, crazy thing is - I'm not allowed in the state of Texas after these past few weeks."

She laughed. We held each other for a few seconds before I offered:

"I'll make coffee… go to bed."

As we embraced, I suddenly pulled away when a massive coyote ran by my leg in the kitchen.

"What the fuck was that?" I asked.

"Oh, that's my mom's cat," she said.

"Your mom… is still here?"

"Yeah, there was a second wave of fires up north. She's staying until Thanksgiving. I figure that was okay."

I went to the pantry and found the first bottle of wine I could grab.

So much for taking time off. ..

THE END

About the Author

Zach Selwyn is an actor/writer/musician originally from Tucson, Arizona. In addition to writing/producing the hit TV show Brainchild on Netflix, he is best known for his History Channel show America's Secret Slang and the groundbreaking Attack of the Show! on G4TV. He has appeared on over 75 programs in the past decade – including writing/producing TBS' digital comedy content, appearing as the House Band Leader on Good Morning Football on NFL Network during the 2019 NFL Draft and hosting and acting in a variety of previous film and TV projects including Sneakerheads, The Mindy Project, Battleship as well as numerous Disney Channel and Discovery Channel shows.

With his band Zachariah & the Lobos Riders, Zach has released six critically acclaimed albums, including the soundtrack to the horror film Dead and Breakfast and 2019's Hacienda which went to number 13 on the Americana Music charts. He has also recorded and performed extensive comedic music and sketches for Comedy Central, Trailer Park Boys and numerous brands across the globe,

Zach initially came to national prominence on the hit ESPN television show "Dream Job" which searched over 20, 000 contestants for the next SportsCenter anchor. Selwyn was tapped by ESPN to host Around the Horn as well as a new pilot, Holla Back in Times Square. He has worked with MLB talent on TBS as well and hosted the live sports trivia show Run The Table in 2020.

Zach is currently writing/developing scripted podcasts for Audio Up Media in Los Angeles, including Totally Hammered: The Legend of Uncle Drank (starring Kinky Friedman), Sonic Leap: Hero the Band, Influencing a Murder and Halloween in Hell.

This is his first novel.